ANOTHER ONE BITES THE CRUST

SPELLBOUND HOUND MAGIC AND MYSTERY BOOK 8

JEANNIE WYCHERLEY

Another One Bites the Crust
Spellbound Hound Magic and Mystery Book 8
BY

JEANNIE WYCHERLEY

Sign up for Jeannie's newsletter: https://www.subscribepage.com/JeannieWycherleyWonky

Another One Bites the Crust was edited by Christine L Baker
Cover design by Cover Affairs.

Formatting by Tammy
Please note: This book is set in England in the United Kingdom.
It uses British English spellings and idioms.

CHAPTER ONE

"You look dapper." Clarissa leaned over and straightened the brand-new ribbon she'd tied around Sal's neck. "That's better."

Toby tried to hide a smirk. Sal, not knowing what dapper meant, rubbed his impressively round belly self-consciously. "She means you look handsome," Toby told him.

"Cor." Sal attempted to flatten down the fur on top of his head. It had a tendency to spike up and Sal preferred it smooth.

"Don't do that," Clarissa said and pushed his paw away. "It looks cute. Punky."

"I'm not sure I want to look cute," Sal muttered, loud enough for only Toby to hear. Not that anyone but Toby could understand him anyway.

"Do I look dapper too?" Toby asked. Clarissa was now peering into her pocket mirror and applying lipstick—black, of course—and seemed to have run out of flattering remarks.

"You shouldn't fish for compliments, Toby," Clarissa said, smooshing her lips together. "It's bad manners."

"I'm not going fishing," said Toby, confused.

Clarissa chuckled, snapped her mirror shut and kissed the top of his head. "You look dashing, as you *always* do!"

Toby beamed at this. *Dashing*. That worked on two levels, didn't it? Dashing as in handsome and dashing as in fast. As a schnauzer-collie-whippet-terrier-thingie he wasn't the speediest furkid on the block, but the whippet part of him meant he could hold his own against ... well, you know, *some* dogs. Terriers. Fat pugs. Twerking corgis. Those kinds of dogs.

But pffft! What did it matter? What he lacked in speed he made up for in smarts.

In Toby's opinion, anyway.

And where Toby was concerned, his opinion was the one that mattered most.

"Dashing," he repeated with satisfaction, filing that away for future use.

"Oh, that's right, Ed. You've had your feet under the table for five minutes and now you're trying to oust us," Toby complained. "Well think on, mister! Clarissa won't stand for that! Will you, Clarissa?" When she didn't immediately answer, Toby cocked his head. "Clarissa?"

"Terrible is the temptation to leave them at home, I know, but Dee Dee specifically asked for Toby to join us as she wants some photos taken with him—"

Toby, who didn't have a clue who Dee Dee was, preened. "Fame at last."

"And it's probably just safer to take Sal along too, don't you think?" Clarissa offered Ed her most winning smile. "After last time."

"Don't remind me," said Ed, rubbing his forehead. For some reason, a few nights previously, while Clarissa and Ed had been out on a date, Sal had taken it upon himself to make a nest in one of Ed's work shoes using the shredded laces and insoles as bedding.

Clarissa tittered.

"Alright." Sighing, Ed reached down and carefully hoisted Sal up, settling him into his jacket's breast pocket. "If you insist. I'll get your lead, shall I?"

Toby nodded in satisfaction. By 'your', Ed presumably meant Clarissa's. Where Toby led, Clarissa followed. It was the natural order of the world.

Honk!

"Taxi's here," Clarissa trilled, entirely unnecessarily. The chances were the whole of Chamberlain Drive was aware of that. There followed a flurry of pocket patting, checking for keys and wallets, lots of jangling and so on, until eventually Clarissa and Ed made it into the back of the taxi with Toby perched between them.

The taxi driver turned his head and gave Toby the evil eye. "He's not gonna barf, is he?" he asked.

"I do beg your pardon," Toby replied primly. "I've already had one of those this morning, thank you."

"Not that kind of barf," Clarissa muttered. Smiling at the driver, she shook her head. "No, don't worry. Honestly. He's great in the car."

Barf in the car? Toby didn't properly understand but he decided to join in the conversation anyway. "I *am* great in the car. I'd be a brilliant driver, me. Better than Clarissa, any day of the week."

"Oi," said Clarissa.

"I'd even make it into third gear from time to time—" Toby continued. "How difficult can it be?"

"Vocal little fellow, ain't he?" The taxi driver turned back to face the road.

"Hahaha," said Ed and clamped a firm arm around Toby's shoulders. "Hush now."

"Where to, folks?" asked the driver.

Clarissa leaned forward. "The Magick Muffin, please."

The driver regarded Clarissa in confusion. "Muffin?"

"The Magick Muffin," Clarissa repeated. "It's a new bakery. Big opening this lunchtime."

"Oh, right, right. New bakery. Yeah, that's on—" The driver fumbled to remember.

"Mayflower Lane," Clarissa finished for him. "One of my university friends is the proprietor."

"Nice. That should spawn an occasional free bun your way, then." The driver performed a zippy four-point turn in the narrow street. Toby found himself glad of Ed's supporting arm.

"I hope so!" Clarissa agreed enthusiastically.

"Nice afternoon out," the driver said. He hadn't come across as particularly cheerful before, but now he sounded properly glum. Toby imagined he'd rather be stuffing his face with cakes than driving people around all afternoon.

"It's work, actually," Clarissa told him. "I'm covering it for my newspaper."

The driver grunted.

"It's not work for me," Ed muttered, but he sounded pleased. "Nice to have a few hours off."

"As long as nobody dies," Toby chipped in. "Because if they do, you'll have to go back in."

Clarissa elbowed him. "Shh!"

"I'm just saying!" Toby protested. "DC Ed wouldn't have a job if people didn't die!"

"We don't have to wish it on anyone!" Clarissa hissed.

The driver glanced in the rearview mirror, evidently unsure whether she was replying to Ed or talking to him. "You can wish a few hours off for me, if you like," he said. "I'd be quite happy to spend lunchtime at a bakery. Will there be freebies?"

"I expect so," said Clarissa.

"I'm counting on it," said Ed.

"Me too!" The very idea of a free meat pie had Toby salivating. "Can you drive a bit faster?" he asked.

CHAPTER TWO

"Clarry!"

A plump lady, the same age as Clarissa and dressed in a pretty, red polka dress of a similar style to Clarissa's, ran up to them as they clambered out of the taxi. While Ed leaned back inside to pay the driver and apologise for Toby's 'singing', Clarissa threw her arms around her friend and gave her a tight squeeze.

"So good to see you again, Dee Dee," she exclaimed. She had to raise her voice to be heard above the sound of the swing quartet performing an upbeat number outside the shop. Pulling away, Clarissa reached for Ed. "This is Ed," she said.

"Pleased to meet you." Ed extended his hand but

Dee Dee was having none of that. She wrapped him up in an equally welcoming hug.

"Lovely to meet you too," she said. "I've heard so much about you—"

Ed raised his eyebrows. "Have you?"

"But not as much as this little chap." Dee Dee knelt down. "You must be Toby!"

"I am, I am—" Toby began to say before he too was crushed under the weight of Dee Dee's embrace. *Blimey!*

"You're too adorable!"

Toby had already warmed to Dee Dee. She obviously recognised quality when she saw it. He extricated himself from her grasp so he could get a better look at her. She had a pale face—rather like Clarissa's—but instead of a goth look, she wore soft, pretty make-up with bright red lips and pink blush. He had to look twice at her eyebrows though; they appeared to have been drawn on with a brown felt tip.

Art, he reminded himself. Face art in this instance.

All around him were people's legs. He had to crane his neck to get a better look at the bakery, festooned with balloons and bunting. Plenty of Union Jacks and ditsy flower prints. Lots of bright colours. The bakery itself had been painted a burnt orange—one of Clarissa's favourite colours—while the mahoosive sign above the window was in purple and decorated with orange pumpkins with wide grins and witches' hats. *The Magick Muffin* it read, in ornate, curly writing. Toby admired it. Properly witchy!

This was a party like no other. The musicians—the swing quartet—were to the side of the bakery's door, squished together because there wasn't a huge amount of room. Several couples—the women's skirts swirling here and there—were doing the Lindy Hop on the cobblestones. Toby didn't know whether these dancers were hired or not, but they were great! He watched as they skipped around, seeing the flash of their white ankle socks in sensible shoes with an occasional glimpse of white underskirt.

Saucy!

He sniffed the air. *Mmmm!* A definite fragrance of sugar and fruit .... Ooh! And the delectable undercurrent of cooked vegetables and meaty pies! *Let there be gravy! Let there be—*

"Congratulations on your new enterprise," Ed was saying. Dee Dee beamed at him and stood up again, her full skirt swishing.

This has to be a theme, Toby decided. *Swishy*

skirts with net petticoats. It's not something you come across every day.

"Thank you so much! It's been a dream of mine to open my own bakery for *yeeeaaarrs*, and finally everything came together and I managed to get a lease on this place. It's so exciting!"

"I have so many questions to ask you!" Clarissa told her. "And I've brought my camera so I can get plenty of shots, but I'll ask our photographer to pop along in the week and take some more professional photos, too!"

"Squeeeeee!" squealed Dee Dee, clapping her hands together. "This is the best day of my life!"

Clarissa laughed at her friend's excitement. Even grumpy Ed—he of the multiple overnight shifts—had lightened up and was smiling and tapping his foot to the music along with everyone else.

"Let me get you some champagne!" Dee Dee said and scurried into the shop.

"I'm totally made up for her!" Clarissa grinned. "She always made the best cakes, all through uni! While the rest of us could barely manage pasta and a tin of tomatoes, she created the most heavenly sponges at the drop of a hat."

"I spent all my money on beer," Ed admitted. "Certainly not on eggs and flour and stuff."

"There is that," Clarissa agreed. "And kebabs after a visit to Rock City." She sighed. "Ahhhh. Them were the days."

"In my day—" Ed had put on a Yorkshire accent. A bad one. Fortunately they never found out what Ed got up to in his day because Dee Dee rejoined them clutching three glasses of fizzy liquid. Toby had high hopes that one of those was for him, but unfortunately it turned out that actually, Dee Dee was hitting the booze too.

"Cheers!" she sang, and clinked glasses with Ed and Clarissa before taking a deep glug. "Oooh, that's good. Still, must behave." She giggled. "I'd better mingle. That's our local MP over there."

Ed grunted.

"And that's Mayor Casterford. I'd better speak to him. I'll catch up with you in a bit, Clarry!" She winked at Ed and waved her fingers in Toby's direction—"Toodles!"—before hurrying off after a man in a suit that had probably cost ten times as much as the one Ed was wearing.

"Phew!" Ed took a deep breath.

"I know." Clarissa laughed. "She's full on, isn't she? Until early evening, that is. She's like a Duracell bunny, keeps on going until her batteries run out and then ends up slumped in front of the TV, half asleep."

"Sounds great, given half the chance," Ed said, twisting his face in a wry grimace. This latest run of night shifts had knocked him for six and he was about ready to sleep for a week.

"Aww, poor you." Clarissa threaded her arm through his. "Let's have a peep inside the shop, shall we? Come on, Tobes."

Toby stuck close to Clarissa's ankles, all the better to avoid being trodden on. The entrance to the bakery had been blocked off with a wide purple ribbon, but they were still able to stand and peer through the window.

"Mmmmmm," said Clarissa.

"Wow," said Ed.

"Yummmmmmmmy!" sang Toby.

"Cor!" said Sal, peering out from his hiding place in Ed's pocket.

Arranged on china serving platters in the window were a range of 'slab' cakes. Unicorn sponge decorated with white lemon icing and hundreds and thousands. Chocolate brownies. Chocolate brownies with caramel. Chocolate brownies with white and dark chocolate swirls. Chocolate brownies with mocha filling. Vanilla brownies. Strudel. Cherry and

"Could I borrow Toby now?" Dee Dee asked.

"Of course." Clarissa handed over the lead and leaned down to kiss his forehead. "Dee Dee wants to have some photos taken with you. Do your best to look cute, okay?"

"That's not difficult when you're as handsome as I am," Toby reminded her and, wagging his tail, trotted happily away.

"Thanks for doing this for me, Toby," Dee Dee said. "I lost my little bestie a few months ago, so it's nice to have some canine company. I miss her dreadfully."

"I'm sorry to hear that," said Toby. Grief is hard. He knew that.

She smiled, gave her head a shake. "These will be the official shots in the local magazine. Think magickal thoughts for me."

And so Toby posed.

This way. That way. This way again. Look up there. What's this? Who's a good boy? Toby knew the drill. In some, Dee Dee twirled an enormous orange umbrella above them both, in others she used it as a prop to lean on while kicking back a leg and holding up one of her impossibly huge muffins as Toby danced in front of her on his back legs. In other shots she cuddled him against her chest while holding a plate of scones—stuffed with clotted cream and strawberry jam, of course—at cheek level, both of them supposedly entranced by the sight.

That didn't require much acting on Toby's part.

Then Toby was placed on a low table covered in a purple tablecloth with pumpkin-decorated paper plates and napkins. More cakes, sausage rolls, pies, pasties and cheese twists, pork pies and other meaty marvels were arranged around him. Irresistible! The photographer took a shot as Toby sniffed the nearest plate.

"Hey!" Toby barked at him. "I wasn't ready!"

"Just like that!" said the photographer. "Maybe a little less angry?"

"What the—?"

"He looks a bit cross," said the photographer.

"This is my resting dog face, you ignoramus," Toby tried to explain.

Dee Dee smoothed the fur beneath his eyes. "Think sweet thoughts," she said. "If you do this right, I've a strawberry shortbread biscuit with your name on it."

"Really?" Toby didn't need telling twice. He looked straight into the camera lens and offered his best beseeching look, channelling his inner I-haven't-been-fed-in-half-a-zillion-years line of thought. Then he changed position and offered his I'm-going-to-die-if-I-don't-eat-soon poses! These were slightly less effective so he switched again, offering smouldering eyes instead. *You cannot deny me. I am your true love.*

He finished with a 'proud alpha canine' pose and was instantly rewarded by a supremely tasty biscuit that did indeed have his name baked into it! T.O.B.Y. *How clever is that?* "I have half a hundredweight of these for you to take home," Dee Dee told him. "I'll give them to Clarissa."

"I wouldn't," Toby replied. "She'll eat them all herself and she won't share a single one with me. She's a meanie."

"I'm sure that's not true," Dee Dee said.

Toby took a step back and stared up at her.

"What? I'm not just cosplaying as a baking witch, you know?" She giggled. "That's why Clarry and I ended up as such good friends. We have a lot in common. Sisters under the moon."

"This is pawesome!" Toby said, his tail whipping back and forth. "I love meeting new witches and wizards. Do you use magick in your bakes?"

Dee Dee winked at him. "Naturally I can't give away my secrets ... but maybe just a sprinkling."

"Wow!"

"Anyway, let me get you back to your pawrents. It's time for me to find the mayor and cut the ribbon."

Ed took charge of Toby while Clarissa located her preferred angle from where to take photos. She arranged herself alongside the photographer and Roddy Higwell, the reporter from the *Sun Valley Tribune*, exchanging curt nods with them both.

No love lost there, thought Toby. But no wonder. Their rotten newspaper had turned its back on the best journalist to ever grace the planet—in Toby's opinion—so it served them right that she had moved on to bigger and better things.

"Hey!" Toby complained when a woman in thick-wedged sandals almost trod on his paw. He glared up at her, although she remained oblivious and continued blocking his view. She had a tattoo on her calf. A butterfly in blue and pink. "Hey!" When she refused to take any notice of him, Toby trod heavily on Ed's foot instead.

Ed peered down. "What's up?"

"I can't see a thing," complained Toby.

"Are you getting crushed?" Ed asked.

Oh boy. "You need to pay more attention during our communication lessons!"

"Here." Ed moved to the edge of the gossiping, excited crowd. They had to crane their necks sideways a little to be able to see, but at least they were out of the way of the wedges, which was a relief to Toby and his delicate tootsies. He wagged his tail and settled himself on Ed's posh shoes. *I'll polish these while I'm down here*, he thought.

The local mayor joined Dee Dee at the door of the bakery, waving and posing with an enormous, oversized pair of orange haberdashery scissors especially commissioned for the occasion, smiling benevolently at the gathering of hungry hordes before leaning in for a series of selfies with locals.

That's the fakest smile I've ever seen, thought Toby. *He'll want a photo with me next.*

The more Toby studied him, the less he liked the man. He was wearing a yellow and brown striped suit with flared trousers and a wide lapel that might have been fashionable at the end of the seventies, along with a mayor's hat plonked on his grey hair and the heavy chain of office hanging around his neck. His teeth were yellow—to match his suit—and there was dandruff on his shoulders.

To add insult to injury, he spent ages simpering with the women who crowded around him, in no rush to perform his duties.

Ed shifted Toby off his shoes and stretched. "Is this thing ever going to get going?" he grumbled, so quietly that only Toby could hear him. "I could have been getting some sleep before my shift later." Toby repositioned himself back on Ed's now shinier shoes.

After much waiting around and a few false alarms—an alarm going off in a nearby shop and a delivery driver needing to get inside The Magick Muffin with some parcels he had for Dee Dee—finally it was time.

"Ladies and gentlemen," Mayor Casterford called in the softest, most ineffectual voice Toby had ever heard, "boys and girls."

"And dogs," said Toby.

Ed wiggled his foot under Toby's rump.

"What?" asked Toby. "It's the 2020s, Ed. We're supposed to be inclusive."

"Ssssh!"

The hubbub died down fractionally, but not to the mayor's satisfaction. He frowned and cleared his throat. "Ladies and gentlemen," he repeated, not much louder than before. Why had nobody thought to set up a microphone and sound system?

Dee Dee was still smiling, but even she was beginning to look a little pained.

Ed sighed and glanced at his watch.

Toby leaned back to look up at him. "Are you famished, Ed? I am."

"I'd kill for one of those muffins ..." Ed muttered.

The mayor tried again. "Ladies and gentlemen."

Dee Dee finally lost patience. "Yo! People!" she bellowed.

Instantly, everyone fell silent.

Ed chuckled. It seemed loud in the sudden quiet, and Clarissa glanced over at him.

Ed turned the chuckle into a cough and thumped his chest.

"Ladies and gentlemen—"

Toby yawned. *This is the most repetitive speech in the history of speeches,* he thought, and stared around at the crowd to see if he could spot anyone he knew. Sun Valley was a relatively small town by British standards and he definitely recognised some faces from visits to the park, but he didn't know anyone to speak to.

No witches, he decided. Just a bunch of cake-loving mundanes. Which seemed fair enough.

A bee buzzed by him as the mayor droned on, blabbering something about community and business and blah blah blooming blah. "Hello, Mr Bee," said Toby, instantly distracted.

The bee zuzzed angrily and darted aggressively towards Toby's head.

Toby ducked. "Hey! Come on, man. I've apologised a million times." While learning magick, back in the early days, he'd accidentally exiled a fair number of bees while practising banishing spells. The problem was he hadn't been able to bring them back because he had absolutely no idea where he'd sent them. "I'm sorry! I'm sorry, okay!"

"Zzzzz!" sang the bee. "Zzzzzzz-zzzzzz!"

Ed peered down at him, wondering what all the fuss was about. "You okay there?"

"Seems I sent Auntie Zzzeeena to certain death or something," Toby told him, but of course, Ed didn't understand a word. "Oopzzzzz."

"You sounded like a bee there for a minute, Tobes," Ed said and guffawed. His timing was rubbish. The mayor had paused to take a breath and once more Ed's mirth filled the sudden silence.

People turned to glare at him with evident disapproval, but worst of all, Clarissa shot him 'a look' that would have cowed Napoleon's army.

"I don't know why they're all staring at us," complained Toby. "They're as bored as we are!"

"Shut up!" Clarissa mouthed at them.

"I think we're in the doghouse," Ed whispered.

Toby's eyebrows twitched. Where was this mythical doghouse? Was it a bad place to be? It sounded pretty cool to him.

"Without further ado, I shall cut the ribbon!" the mayor announced, and there was a universal cheer as he wielded his enormous scissors and the ribbon fell away gracefully. "All that remains is for us to fill our bellies. I pronounce The Magick Muffin ... open!"

"Hooray!" yelled Ed, then much more quietly inserted, "About time."

"No more speeches!" Toby added his voice to the sudden mayhem. People began to push and shove to get towards the shop door.

"Take your time," Dee Dee called. "There's plenty for everyone!"

"I sure hope so." Ed sighed. "We'll have to wait for Clarissa to finish what she's doing anyway, so we're going to be at the back of the queue."

"What?" Sal poked his head out of Ed's pocket. "I'm fading away in here! Can't you hear my stomach rumbling?"

Ed hurriedly pushed the rat's snout out of sight.

"Disaster," Toby agreed, and hunkered down beside Ed to stare moodily at the famished masses ahead of them. "I hope they leave something for us."

"They'd better!" Sal warned, his voice muffled. "Otherwise I'll set my mates on them."

"You don't have any mates," Toby reminded him.

"Harsh!" said Sal. "Harsh!"

CHAPTER THREE

"Why did you decide to move to Sun Valley?" Clarissa asked, pen poised over her notepad. It was late in the afternoon and the bakery was now closed. Ed and Clarissa were sitting at a table in the corner while Dee Dee washed plates and trays and wiped down counters. Given that Clarissa was distracted by interviewing Dee Dee for her *Celestine Times* article and Ed had his face buried in the world's largest muffin, Toby busily hoovered up crumbs from the floor free of human disapproval for a change.

Dee Dee giggled. "Having visited my long-time best friend here, I know what a beautiful part of the world it is. There are some fabulous independent shops with several delis and a couple of other artisan bakers, so it seemed like a great place to base myself."

"You don't think there's too much competition?" Ed asked, wiping a smear of mocha chocolate ganache from his top lip.

Clarissa gave him a look that might have shrivelled a grape.

"What?" Ed protested. "I'm just wondering whether it's possible to have too many bakeries, that's all. Sun Valley is a small town."

Toby glanced up momentarily. "Too many bakeries? That's not even a thing ..." *Ooh! Hang on! A slither of iced topping ... I just need to get this ...*

Dee Dee grinned. "My point of view is, if you have a number of similar businesses in the same vicinity, that seems to suggest there's a demand within the community for similar items. Not the *same*," she emphasised, "but *similar*."

Ed regarded her doubtfully, then shrugged and took another bite of his football-sized muffin.

"That brings me to my next question," Clarissa said, scribbling in her notebook. "What makes The Magick Muffin different to the other bakeries in Sun Valley? Why should people choose you over the competition?"

Dee Dee raised a hand. "I'm going to stop you

there, Clarry. We shouldn't see the other wonderful bakeries in Sun Valley as competition. Surely they are an intrinsic part of consumer choice? The way I see it, when you have six or seven bakeries all serving up the most delectable goodies—"

"Definitely delectables," said Toby.

"—you are totally spoilt. The customer gets to throw their head back"—Dee Dee demonstrated by doing just that and scratching her chin with her index finger—"and ponder. Hmmm, they'll think. What do I fancy today? And rather than selecting from one menu, they have the combined might of six or seven menus. One day they might fancy something Italian from one bakery, another day they'll choose a custard slice from the bakery on the market—"

Wow, thought Toby. *She's done her homework.*

"And then the next day, they'll decide they want a magick muffin. There's room for all of us!"

Clarissa smiled at this. "And are the muffins magick?"

Dee Dee grinned. "As I told Toby, I really can't give away my trade secrets."

"Ahem!"

No-one had heard the door open. The mayor was

standing there, his face twisted into something of a smile.

"Ooh!" Dee Dee clutched her heart. "I didn't see you there!"

"All good?" the mayor asked, his eyes scanning the bakery, taking in Ed with his chocolatey face and Clarissa with her notebook. "I brought your mug back. Thank you for the tea."

"No problem." Dee Dee reached for it.

The mayor frowned at Toby. Toby wagged his tail. "Do you allow dogs in this establishment?" he asked, his voice grave with disapproval.

"Only this particular dog," Dee Dee replied cheerfully. "He's my mascot."

Clarissa reached down and clicked her fingers at Toby.

Toby—offended—regarded the fingers, debating whether to lick them or bite them off. He decided, for the sake of long-term peace, to ignore them. He turned his back on Clarissa and continued sniffing around the floor in search of more offerings.

"What about rats?" the mayor asked.

"Rats?" Dee Dee asked, and now she seemed uncertain.

"Like that one." The mayor pointed at a rat

sitting on a tray on the counter, tucking into a cheese straw almost as large as he was.

Dee Dee shrieked. Quick as a flash, Ed abandoned his muffin and jumped up. Reaching for the rat—either too stuffed or too stunned to move—he scooped it up and shoved it into his jacket pocket. "I'm so sorry about that!"

"Ed!" Clarissa glared at him.

"What—?" Dee Dee clamped her hands against her cheeks.

"It's my rat. My fault. He's a pet!" Ed explained, evidently willing to take the fallout.

"Ed—" Clarissa tried to jump in but Ed shushed her before explaining to the mayor. "I brought him along because I thought he'd enjoy the outing." He shrugged and turned to Dee Dee. "Sorry, Dee Dee! Entirely my fault."

Dee Dee gagged. "You brought a rat into my bakery?"

"To be fair, he's a very well-behaved rat," Ed tried to explain.

"A model citizen," said Toby, studying Ed's bulging pocket with interest.

"And he had a bath this morning," Clarissa chipped in.

The mayor curled his lip. "You gave the rat a bath?"

"It was more of a shower," said Clarissa. "He'd drown in the bath."

"Huhuhuh." The mayor tried to laugh, but judging by his face, he was completely disgusted.

Dee Dee hurried out from behind the counter with a cardboard box tied up with orange and purple ribbon. "I prepared these for you and your wife, Mayor Casterford." She held the box out.

The mayor didn't take it from her. "Cakes?"

"A selection of my bakes, yes." Dee Dee nodded.

"Made in *this* bakery?" The mayor's voice sounded strained.

"Yes." Dee Dee's reply was little more than a whisper.

"No, thank you," said the mayor and, turning on his heel, marched away.

The bakery fell silent. Dee Dee's eyes filled with tears.

Ed's head dropped. Clarissa's lower lip wobbled. She hurried to Dee Dee and wrapped her arms around her. "I'm so sorry," she said. "This is my fault, not Ed's. I brought Sal along, not him."

"Well—" Ed stepped up, ever gallant, but Clarissa scowled at him and he shut up.

"You have a pet rat?" Dee asked, her voice hitching.

"I think he's more Toby's pet than mine," Clarissa admitted.

Toby's magnificent eyebrows twitched. "Erm—"

They were interrupted by muffled squeaking. "You'll 'ave to get out!" Sal was shouting. "This is my pocket!"

Ed peered down at his chest. His breast pocket bulged and juddered. Sal sounded furious. "What are you doing in 'ere anyway? Get out, get out, get OUT!"

A rat's head poked up from the pocket. "I was ratnapped!" he shrieked.

Toby cocked his head. Whoever that rat was, he wasn't Sal.

This was confirmed almost immediately, when Sal popped up beside him, still wearing the bow Clarissa had tied around his neck, although looking distinctly more dishevelled now. "I'd like to protest!" he yelled. "I'm an *only* rat, int I? I didn't sign up to share space with a common or garden street urchin!"

The newcomer flared his nostrils in Sal's direction. "How very dare you! I'm a house rat! I live in *this* building! I've always lived in this building. As have my ancestors. Way back before this place was an auto repairs shop till when it was a greengrocer's. In fact—"

"What are they saying?" Clarissa asked Toby.

"Sal's not happy that Ed has started a new collection of friends without his permission," Toby translated, taking a little liberty with the truth.

Ed stared down at his hands, completely aghast. "Did I just pick up a rat?"

"You've picked up rats before," said Clarissa, reaching for his pocket.

"But-but—"

"What's the difference?" Clarissa scooped the spare rat up.

"Waaaah!" Ed pulled a face and backed away.

Clarissa turned the rat over to get a good look at it, then turned to Dee Dee. "What would you like me to do with it?"

"Maybe we'd better put it out in the street."

"It lives here," Toby pointed out. "You'd be making it homeless."

The rat, swinging ineffectually in Clarissa's grasp, threw punches towards her. "I'll find my way back in," he squeaked.

"No problem, mate! Course you will!" said Sal, nodding in approval. Now that the interloper had been removed from his immediate vicinity, he felt safe enough to take its side.

Clarissa and Dee Dee exchanged looks before Dee Dee sighed and leaned closer to the rat. She placed a finger on its forehead and it became still. "Listen to me," she told it, in a soft voice. "Here's the deal. You can stay here in the bakery on two conditions. Are you listening?"

The rat's black eyes met hers.

"You never, never, NEVER show yourself to another human except to me ever again. Right?"

The rat squeaked.

"And you never, ever, ever eat from anything on my counters, shelves or in my pantry. Got it?"

This time the rat stared at her askance. Before it could squeak a refusal of the terms, Sal piped up. "You're gonna let him starve, are you?"

Toby took up Sal's argument. "Sal says—"

"I know what Sal says," Dee Dee told him. Toby blinked. Dee Dee could speak rat as well as dog. *Wow! Think on that, Clarissa!* "Fear not, little one. I'll leave you your supper in a bowl before I lock up every night."

The rat squeaked softly and began to clean its whiskers. Dee Dee reached out and took him from Clarissa. "I think we have a deal," she said, and leaned over to free the little fellow. He scampered away behind the door, leaving them to their business.

As Dee Dee straightened up, Clarissa glanced at the open door. "What are we going to do about the mayor?" she asked. "What if he starts telling people that The Magick Muffin is overrun by rodents?"

Dee Dee rolled her eyes. "Leave him to me."

CHAPTER FOUR

Toby raised his head and blinked. Somewhere in the house a phone was ringing. Clarissa's mobile one, not the big phone. From the bedroom next door, he heard the sound of a thump: Clarissa knocking something off her nightstand.

What time is it? It doesn't feel like getting-up time. Not yet. Toby slid, a little reluctantly, off Old Joe's bed. This is where he liked to sleep most nights, on top of the bed Old Joe had once shared with him. These days, there was no Old Joe, but his jumper remained, folded neatly on the pillows, and Toby would sniff it from time to time. It brought him comfort.

Once up, Toby was of course fully awake. He

trotted into Clarissa's room to find her hanging upside down and swinging her arm under the bed.

"Who was on the phone?" Toby asked.

"I have no idea," Clarissa said, her voice muffled. "I dropped it and now I can't find it." She threw herself upright, her tousled hair sticking up at odd angles, her face flushed. "Can you have a look?"

Toby baulked at this. "Under the bed?"

"I think that's where it went."

"Uh-uh." Toby took a step back.

"What?" Clarissa pushed her hair back off her forehead. "Why not?"

"Monsters."

She shook her head. "There are no monsters under the bed, Tobes."

"Dust devils," Toby told her.

Clarissa closed her eyes. "Dust devils?"

"Fierce, evil creatures."

"Is that right?" Sighing, Clarissa swung her legs out of bed and dangled her feet over the side.

"Watch out. They'll bite your toes!" Toby warned her and danced out onto the landing, barking at the creatures under the bed.

"Sssh!" Clarissa waved at him. "You'll wake Mrs Crouch!"

Mrs Crouch was their adjoining neighbour.

Noise wasn't generally a problem because the houses had been built in the 1930s when soundproofing had been top-notch. They heard the occasional thump, but not much more than that.

Clarissa yawned. "What time is it anyway?" she asked when Toby had calmed down enough for her to get a word in.

"You'll have to rescue your phone from the dust devils to find out for sure," said Toby, keeping a careful eye out for movement.

"Hmm." Clarissa eased herself onto the rug beside the bed and peered underneath. "It is a bit dusty under here," she admitted, pushing aside an ancient suitcase that lived there. "I can't see it. Where is it?"

Groaning, she lay flat on the floor and stretched her hand as far as it would go. Toby couldn't resist—he joined her, his head pressed against hers. "Watch out for the monsters," he said and began licking her face.

Clarissa yelped and tried to push him away. "How is that helping?" Her struggles only made things worse. Toby became more excited and keen to share his kisses. "Get off!" Clarissa began to giggle. "Ugh! Get off!"

From downstairs came the trilling of the big

phone. Toby stopped what he was doing and cocked his head.

"What's going on this morning?" Clarissa asked, pushing herself to her feet and swiping at her now expertly washed visage. "Did someone die?"

"Whoa!" Toby regarded her in admiration. "How witchy of you!"

"I'm not saying someone *did* die." Clarissa pulled at her t-shirt and stepped past him to run downstairs. Toby followed, easily keeping up, his snout pressed to the back of her knee. "It's a figure of speech!"

She scooped up the receiver and juggled it for a moment before situating it in the proper place beside her mouth and ear. "Hello?"

Toby heard a shrill voice gabbling but couldn't make out what was being said.

"Huh?" Clarissa asked. "Sorry. Yes. Just—"

More shrillness.

"Rowena. Slow down. I—"

The voice—of Rowena Gubbens, Clarissa's boss—didn't slow down. Neither did it become less strident.

"Rowena! I've literally just woken up. What are you talking about?"

Finally, the message seemed to get through to Rowena. She must have turned the volume down because now Toby could hear nothing whatsoever. Clarissa listened, frowning. At intervals she interspersed with comments such as "How?" or "Really?" or "You're joking!" or "Oh dear!" and finally, "You know I only saw him yesterday, right?"

Toby pricked his ears up at this and rapidly cycled through all the hims he knew. Himself, of course. Ed. *Wha—?* He took a sharp intake of breath. Ed is dead? No. It couldn't be. He had a feeling that Clarissa would be much more upset if Ed had turned up his toes!

Sal then? *Oh, dogness! Has something happened to Sal?* Without waiting to hear more from Clarissa, Toby scuttled into the kitchen and leapt through the dog flap. Sal slept in Toby's wizarding shed so Toby knew exactly where he ought to be. He nuzzled open the door and stared into the shadows.

He could see his old dog basket. He hadn't actually finished with this basket, but Sal had shredded a large part of it and had therefore claimed it as his own, resulting in Clarissa having to buy Toby a new one. And there was Sal, nestled up, nose to tail, looking perfectly cosy and peaceful. Toby, holding his breath, crept inside and nudged the fat rat.

Sal jumped to attention, his little face a rictus grimace of fear. When he comprehended who'd woken him up, he glared at his friend. "Hey! What's the meaning of this? Get outta here!"

"Sorry, bud." Toby breathed an audible sigh of relief. "I thought you were a goner!"

"Agonner?" Sal eyed him suspiciously. "Who's he? Or is it a she?"

"Never mind." Toby turned to go.

"Is that it? You've woken me up over a case of mistaken identity?"

"I was checking you were ... Never mind!" Toby shook his head, exasperated. "I don't know why you're complaining. I thought rats were nocturnal."

"We're whatever we wanna be, and at the moment what I wanna be is asleep!" Sal threw himself down onto the soft basket and closed his eyes.

Toby wasn't worried about being summarily dismissed in such a way; he wanted to get back to Clarissa and find out exactly which 'him' she'd been referring to. Given the number of people she'd spoken to at the launch of The Magick Muffin, it could be any of them. Toby dived back through the dog flap and hurried to Clarissa's side. She was now sitting cross-legged on the hallway floor with the phone jammed between her ear and her shoulder while making notes in her trusty notepad.

"Okay, I'm on it," she said and hung up.

"What's going on?" Toby asked her.

"We-eeeeeeell!" Clarissa exhaled, drawing the word out. "All hell has broken loose!"

"*What*?" Toby's eyes widened. "Oh no! Demon apocalypse!" He rushed to the front door to check it was locked and bolted and that the safety chain was across it as it should be. "Do we have enough supplies?"

"Enough supplies?" Clarissa brushed her right hand through her fringe to get it out of her eyes and managed to tangle the lid of her biro in her hair. "For heaven's sake, what's going on here—"

"If we're going to be holed up in here while the forces of good and evil fight each other, we'll need supplies," Toby said, thinking quickly. "Bottled water. Dog snacks. Toilet roll."

Clarissa shook her head. "I need a cuppa." She padded through to the kitchen.

"Good idea! Tea bags!" *Hoomans can't survive without tea,* Toby remembered. *Even zombie ones.*

Clarissa groaned. "It's not even six o'clock yet."

"Or maybe we should go somewhere secure," Toby said, following her. "What do you think? An underground bunker somewhere? But if we're taking Sal it had better not be down a sewer because

I don't think his old mafia family have forgiven him yet—"

"What are you talking about, Toby?" Clarissa set down her notebook and reached for the kettle.

"Ooh! A better idea! Why don't we go and join Ed at the police station? They'll have supplies and the means to protect us!" Toby checked his bowl. It was disappointingly empty. Still, there would have to be rationing now that the end of the world was upon them. It was to be expected.

"Ed's not at the police station." Clarissa reached for the tea caddy. "Someone burned it down, remember?"

Oops.

"Or rather, he's in a portacabin in the car park that passes as a police station but isn't really ..."

"What's a portacabin?" Toby asked.

"It's a temporary building. I think they're usually constructed from cardboard and two-ply. They're a bit flimsy."

"Are they?" Toby reconsidered their apocalypse options. "So, we don't want to hide there. We'd better stay here."

"What are you going on about?" Clarissa was getting irritated now. Probably through the stress of it all, Toby decided.

"If hell has broken loose we'll need to hide from the demons!"

"Hell? Demons? What?" Clarissa looked perplexed for a second, but then sudden understanding illuminated her face. She closed her eyes and sighed. "Oh, Toby. You can be quite literal sometimes."

Toby regarded her suspiciously. "Is that a good thing?"

"It's a *you* thing." Clarissa chuckled and leaned over to scratch between his ears. "Hell is staying right where it is, don't worry. Although ... I'm not sure which side we'd be on anyway ..." She reached for her mug from the draining board and dropped a teabag inside.

"On the side of the righteous, obviously!" Toby cried, striking a pose with his nose in the air.

"Mmm. Well anyway, as I was saying, all hell ... no ... let's rephrase that. There's been a bit of a furore—"

"Furry orgy?"

"No! A ... a ... murder! There's been a murder!"

"Has there? Why didn't you say so?" Toby asked. "Anyone we know?"

"Toby!" Clarissa frowned at him. "That's a terrible thing to ask."

"I want to know whether I'm grieving or not," Toby argued. "And if so, where would it be on the scale?"

"The scale?" The kettle finally began to whistle; Clarissa turned to it and began pouring steaming water into her mug.

"Yes, you know. Old Joe is worth ten on my scale and The Pointy Woman is worth minus ten." Toby sniffed. "Minus ten hundred, even."

"Right, I see. Hmmm. According to my boss, the victim is Mayor Casterford."

Ah! The 'him' from yesterday. Toby wrinkled his snout, considering how he felt about this news. He had to push aside some hunger pangs to do this. The mayor hadn't seemed a particularly pleasant person, but on the other hand, what had he done to deserve—

Clarissa caught her breath, her eyes meeting Toby's.

"Are you thinking what I'm thinking?" Toby asked.

Clarissa clamped a hand to her chest as though she was suffering a sudden heart attack. "Dee Dee! What she said about taking care of the mayor ... it could be misconstrued!"

"No, I was wondering what time breakfast is,"

Toby told her. "It was a good guess though. That was probably my next thought—"

"We have to go." Clarissa pulled her travel mug out of the cupboard.

"Go where?"

"Go and see Dee Dee." She poured the contents of her porcelain mug into the travel mug and added another splash of boiling water for good measure.

"What about my breakfast?"

"I'll pack something to take with us. Come on! Let's get moving!" Then she was gone, hightailing it upstairs to dive into the shower and get dressed.

Toby's stomach growled. Breakfast had been so near and yet so far, and of course, now that he'd considered it more seriously, he *was* famished. Sighing, he stared pointedly at the cupboard next to the one under the sink and wished the door open. It obliged. Once that was done, it was an easy matter to open up the tub where his biscuit mix was stored. Opening a can was slightly more complex but he'd had a lot of practice, much to Clarissa's dismay. There'd been a period of a few weeks when, every time she'd arrived home, Toby would have half the contents of the pantry out, having been experimenting with different ways to use a can opener.

That had been messy. He was so much better at it now.

He directed all of his attention to choosing a flavour for his breakfast. "Lamb and carrot," he decided—given that frying bacon and sausage would have been a step too far and might have seen him rehomed—and so, by the time Clarissa came back downstairs, clasping her dusty phone with its scratched screen while the rest of her was all clean and sweetly scented, Toby had eaten enough food to tide him over for ... at least ten minutes.

"Ready?" she called from the hallway.

"Ready," said Toby, and helpfully levitated her notebook and travel mug out of the kitchen to join her near the front door. "Don't forget these!"

"Phew!" Clarissa swung her ridiculously oversized battered handbag over one shoulder. It contained her camera, pens, tissues, sweets, poo bags and dog treats, so was therefore an exceedingly important part of her wardrobe. "What would I do without you?"

"Let's hope you never have to find out," Toby replied and smartly trotted out of the front door ahead of her. "Don't forget your lead!"

"*Your* lead!" Clarissa muttered.

"I lead, you follow," Toby called over his

shoulder before turning and winking at Moriarty, the black cat from across the road, who had taken up residence on his gatepost. "Need to keep these hoomans in check," he told her.

"Always," purred Moriarty, her bright green eyes glinting. "And what are you up to today, pray tell? Arranging the demise of more of your enemies?"

"Good grief, no!" Toby declared. "Today, I'm solving a murder!"

Moriarty made a snuffling noise that might have been a laugh or might have been her attempting to dislodge a mouse's thigh bone from her throat. It was difficult to tell where Moriarty was concerned.

"Just another pleasant Sun Valley Sunday, then," she said.

"See you later for some twilight barking?" Toby asked.

Moriarty nodded once. "You can tell me all about it then."

CHAPTER FIVE

Clarissa tapped on the door of the bakery but to no avail. Inside, the shop remained in darkness and the door through to the rear firmly closed.

"I can't smell anything baking," Toby told her.

"It's Sunday," Clarissa said, as though that explained anything.

Toby frowned. "So it is." He lifted his nose. The sour smell of stale beer from the nearby pub floated on the breeze. He could also smell bacon sizzling, but that came from a variety of directions in the distance. Nowhere close. There was toast as well. "No baking," he repeated.

"The bakery isn't open on a Sunday," Clarissa replied, tapping on the door once more.

"Not open?" *Madness!* "Doesn't anyone want fresh bread on a Sunday? What about croissants?" Old Joe had been partial to a buttery croissant.

"They'd probably appreciate it but a baker needs at least one day off, don't they?"

"I suppose so," Toby replied, sounding doubtful. Given that The Magick Muffin had only opened the day before, he couldn't imagine that Dee Dee needed much downtime yet.

"I think we'll have to go around the back," Clarissa said, and Toby dutifully led her down the road and up the side street until they came to the alley that ran behind the row of shops. Clarissa counted the premises until they came to one with a pile of empty flour bags outside the back door and a heap of collapsed cardboard boxes addressed to The Magick Muffin. "This is the one. We need to go up the steps."

The steps were made of iron and clanged as Clarissa began to climb them. Toby followed, treading carefully. He didn't like the open aspects of the stairs and, to add fuel to the fire, even the treads had been created with patterned holes in them, probably to make them lighter to assemble. They were worse than the ladder stairs attached to his wizard shed. By the time he scaled them, Clarissa was already standing outside the door and knocking. She carried on knocking until eventually a dark shadow loomed behind the mottled glass and they heard the sound of the security chain being drawn.

"Clarry?" Dee Dee peered out through the tiniest of gaps, her voice husky and her eyes full of sleep. "What time is it?"

"A little after seven," Clarissa told her. "Can I come in?"

Dee Dee's brow creased, but she held open the door and allowed Clarissa and Toby to step inside. "What's going on? It's a little early for a social call on a Sunday."

"I'm really sorry to disturb you. I'm guessing you haven't heard the news?" Clarissa wrinkled her nose. "Let's put the kettle on, shall we?"

Always the kettle, thought Toby. *Why can't anyone do anything without making a cup of tea?*

"Sure." Dee Dee cleared her throat and led the way into the apartment proper. It was small and cosy. To the right as you came in was a galley kitchen that looked out over the rear aspect of the town. It wasn't much of a view, just rooftops and industrial buildings, old warehouses, that kind of thing. Next to the kitchen was a door that probably led into the bathroom, but it was closed so Toby couldn't have a nose around. Then the 'hallway'—such as it was—opened up into one large studio space that was both bedroom and living room. There was some semblance of order in here, in that the bed had been organised and there was a desk with a computer, but boxes were piled high on the dining table and the sofa was covered in clothes.

Dee Dee shuffled over to the window—a massive bay that looked out onto Mayflower Lane—and pulled open the curtains. "I apologise for the mess," she said, scooping up armfuls of clothes and depositing them on her bed. "I've been concentrating on the shop and I haven't managed to get around to sorting my own living space out."

"Don't worry," Clarissa said. "I've seen worse."

"At least it's not smelly," agreed Toby.

"Thanks for that, Toby." Clarissa leaned over and unclipped her lead.

Symbolic, Toby decided. *She wants to detach herself from my comment.*

"So, what's up? What's this visit about?" Dee Dee indicated a freshly cleared space on the sofa and Clarissa plonked herself down.

"There's no easy way to say this so I'll just come right out with it. I heard from Rowena this morning, she's my boss at *The Celestine Times*.

Word had just come into the paper that—" Clarissa paused, before evidently deciding to purge herself. Her words fell out, garbling into the silence. "Word had come into the newsroom that the mayor of Sun Valley was dead. Probably murdered. And I thought about what you said yesterday and figured I'd better come and talk to you about it before someone else does."

Dee Dee, frowning, sat heavily on the edge of her bed. "Mayor Casterford?"

"Yes."

"Dead?"

"Yes."

"Probably murdered?"

"That's what Rowena said. Whether she was basing that conclusion on the fact that his death was sudden and unexpected or something else, I don't know."

"How did he die?"

Clarissa shrugged. "I don't know."

Dee Dee blinked her eyes rapidly before leaning forward and putting her head in her hands. Clarissa and Toby watched. When Dee Dee sat up again, her eyes were wide and her shock had given way to fear. "Do *you* think *I* did it?"

"Oh, gosh, no!" Clarissa jumped to her feet and

rushed over to hug her friend. "Of course we don't, do we, Toby?"

Until this moment, with Clarissa putting him on the spot, Toby hadn't honestly given it much thought. Sitting in front of the sofa, on Dee Dee's winter coat, he regarded the two women astutely. *If I say 'of course not', that won't be an intellectual response,* thought Toby, *but if I say 'I don't know', that will get me into trouble.*

"Any chance of a biscuit?" he asked.

"All he ever thinks about is his stomach," said Clarissa, giving Dee Dee's arm a squeeze.

Dee Dee managed a watery smile. "Let me see what I have in the kitchen—"

"Anything cheesy would go down a treat," Toby told her.

"I'll make coffee while I'm at it. Clarry?"

"Yes." Clarissa smiled. "That would be lovely."

"Okay. Give me a moment." Dee Dee disappeared into her kitchen. They listened to the sound of water running, and then a moment later she slipped into the bathroom and closed the door behind her.

Clarissa made her way back over to the sofa. Reaching down, she rubbed Toby's head. "Any chance of a biscuit?" she hissed. "What was that about? You can't seriously believe Dee Dee would hurt anyone."

"I don't know her as well as you do," Toby admitted. "But we heard what she said yesterday. 'Leave it to me', she said!"

"Leave *him* to me," Clarissa corrected him, then caught herself and sighed. "But that's not what she meant."

"If you were one hundred per cent convinced that that's not what she meant, then we wouldn't be having this conversation right now," Toby pointed out.

"You're impossible!" Clarissa sounded upset, but Toby recognised that for once *he* wasn't the cause—it was only that she found herself doubting her friend.

"It's not me you need to worry about," said Toby.

"What do you mean?"

Toby glanced towards the rear of the apartment. They could hear the kettle humming. As if on cue, there came a smart rapping at the door.

Clarissa jumped. "Who's that?" She didn't immediately move until the rapping came again. It sounded a little more impatient now. Clarissa half stood as Dee Dee emerged from the bathroom. "Do you want me to get it?" she asked. Dee Dee was still in her pyjamas.

"No, no, it's fine. Someone else arriving to join the party," she joked. She disappeared from view. Clarissa sat down again and placed one hand on Toby's head. They listened to the sound of the door opening.

"Ed!" exclaimed Dee Dee. "You must have heard me put the kettle on."

"Hi, Dee Dee," came Ed's voice. "Sorry to disturb you so early in the morning—"

"Don't worry, come in."

"This isn't a social call, I'm afraid." Ed sounded awkward.

"Why am I not surprised. I have a couple of your friends here already."

"Friends?"

"Yes, *friends*!" Toby barked.

"Is that Toby?" Ed sounded surprised. A second later, he appeared before them, blinking in surprise to see Clarissa perched on the sofa.

"Hey," she said.

"Hey." He moved further into the room, navigating around a pile of boxes. When Toby wagged his tail, Ed knelt beside him to give him some love. Peering up at Clarissa, he shook his head. "What are you doing here?"

"The same as you, I suspect," said Clarissa. "Chasing a story."

"What story would that be?" Ed asked cautiously.

Clarissa gazed up at him from under her eyelashes, her lips pursed.

"Ah." Realisation flooded Ed's face. "Good news travels fast, doesn't it?"

Dee Dee had followed him in, tugging self-consciously at her pyjama top. "That's what we're calling it, are we? Good news?"

Ed turned to her. "No, of course not. Not at all." He took a breath. "I came here as a friend, Dee Dee, as soon as I heard the news." He shifted uncomfortably.

"Am I being investigated?" Dee Dee asked.

"I'd guess it's a matter of time," Ed answered delicately. "There hasn't been an autopsy yet, but ... er ... initial indications are that the mayor ingested poison."

"Poison?" Dee Dee's face paled.

Ed held his hands up. "Let's not jump to conclusions—"

"Might he have taken it himself?" Clarissa asked, notebook in hand.

Ed frowned at her. "Don't be quoting me in any

article you write. You'll get me into trouble, and I could do without going through that again!"

"Yes! He might have taken it himself!" Dee Dee clung to the suggestion as though it were a lifebuoy.

"Anything is possible," Ed agreed, but he sounded doubtful.

"He can't have eaten poison at the launch yesterday," Toby said, "otherwise we'd all be dying, and so far—" He checked himself out. Everything appeared to be where it usually was and was the same colour as normal, although given the fleck of his coat, it was difficult to tell ... "we're all still alive." He stared up at Ed—who'd come here straight from his night shift—and noted the dark shadows under his eyes. "Most of us, anyway."

"That's true," said Clarissa, relaying Toby's input to Ed. "You'll need to check with everyone else who came to the launch yesterday, including us. None of us seem to have been affected."

Ed nodded. "At the moment this isn't my case. Come this evening when I'm back on duty, it may well be." He smiled apologetically at Dee Dee. "If I were you I wouldn't touch anything in the bakery. If there's a rational explanation for all this, then the investigating team will find it. It's easier all round if you leave everything as it is."

"Oh." Tears welled up in Dee Dee's eyes. "This is a nightmare."

"We'll get to the bottom of it, don't worry," Ed said, and Clarissa nodded sagely.

Hmmm, thought Toby, *I'm sure I could be more than helpful in this regard. Let me see what I can do!*

CHAPTER SIX

Ed had disappeared back to his own home shortly after that exchange to get some sleep before heading back to work later. He wasn't fond of night shifts, but he, like every other police officer in the land, was required to do a number of them every month. A necessary evil. Criminals don't operate on a nine-to-five, after all.

Toby tried to slink downstairs into the shop, but Clarissa caught him before he could reach the stairs and soon put paid to that. "What do you think you're doing?" she asked.

"Investigating," he told her. *Der. Isn't it obvious?*

"The police don't need you poking around where you shouldn't be," she scolded.

Toby faced up to her. "Admit it. You desperately want to take a look too!"

"There's nothing to see." Dee Dee had spent some time in the bathroom, ostensibly taking a shower and getting changed, but judging by her red-rimmed eyes, she'd been crying too. "Look, I can take you down there—"

"No." Clarissa spoke firmly. "Let's wait for the police to make their next move, if they're going to make one. We don't want to be charged with tampering with evidence or ..."—she narrowed her eyes in Toby's direction—"sniffing or eating the evidence!"

Eat the evidence? "As if I would," Toby huffed. *Honestly.* "Of course, I'd have to *sniff* the evidence. That's the whole point of police dogs. I'm PD Silverwind."

"PD? You're *not* a police dog," Clarissa replied archly.

"I'm a detective," Toby said.

"In your dreams."

"A great wizarding detective."

"Detectives go through training—"

"I've been trained!"

"As a wizard. And only partially—"

Hmmm. She has a point. "I'm a private detective.

PD stands for private detective. I'm a WPD. Wizarding private detective." Or … "Maybe WPDCD. Wizarding private detective, canine division."

"Whatever." Clarissa gave up.

"I'll make us some more coffee," said Dee Dee and disappeared into the kitchen.

"I'm already bouncing off the walls," Clarissa muttered, but she understood Dee Dee needed something to do. In times of crisis, don't we all?

Sighing, she went to the window and peered out. There were a few people in the street now, some walking their dogs, others clutching newspapers or coffees. The café up the road had opened and was serving breakfast. Church bells were ringing in the distance. An ordinary Sunday morning to all intents and purposes.

But not for Dee Dee.

And certainly not for Mayor Casterford.

"You don't have to hang around, you know." Dee Dee reappeared clutching a cluttered tray containing two small pottery mugs, a cafetière full of freshly brewed coffee, some recently baked biscotti and a small jug of milk.

"I know," Clarissa said, wrapping her arms around her chest in a self-hug. "It's awkward, isn't it?

I'm here because I'm a journalist and my editor sent me, but at the same time you're my best mate and I want to support you."

Dee Dee set the tray down on the floor. There wasn't anywhere else. Toby wandered over to inspect the biscotti. Clarissa shooed him away. "You know, while I'm here, why don't I help you organise a bit?"

Dee Dee scowled around at the chaos. "I can't ask you to do that."

"Oh, I love tidying," Clarissa lied.

"Well, I was going to give it a go today," Dee Dee admitted.

"Exactly!" Clarissa slapped her palms together. "Where shall I start?"

Dee Dee pointed out a number of boxes piled haphazardly in the corner. "Those are books and photos and things. If you could maybe arrange the books on the shelves—"

"I love books!" Clarissa sang happily. "How do you like them arranged? Alphabetically? By size? By colour?"

"Any old how," said Dee Dee.

"Really?" Clarissa looked slightly scandalised by this. She was fastidious about her non-fiction books being arranged by subject and her fiction books being alphabetic.

"Mm-hm." Dee Dee had crouched next to her bed and was pulling out a suitcase. "I'll get started on my clothes."

"We'll get through this lot in no time," Clarissa said.

Toby scanned the room. He wasn't so sure. There was a lot of 'stuff'. It looked like Dee Dee had downsized from a four-bed house somewhere. He began to inch away from the women, hopeful that Clarissa would remain otherwise engaged. When she paid him no attention, he skedaddled out into the hall and down the stairs to the shop.

Where there had once been carpet on the stairs, this had been removed and only the odd spiky nail remained, threatening to ambush his plans. He trod carefully and quietly until he reached the ground floor and the old, cold, black and white chequered tiles that had probably been in situ for over a hundred years. There was a door to the left, the shop itself, and a door to the right, the storeroom, no doubt. Both doors were closed and the shop door had been locked, but that posed no problem for the ever-resourceful WPDCD Toby Silverwind.

Where to start?

Wagging his tail, he waved a paw, unlocked the door into the shop and pushed it open, stepping into the light, airy space to be enveloped in the heavenly perfumes of chocolate and vanilla, scents so thick he could have carved off a piece of each and eaten them.

"Oooh. Yum!"

The bakery looked more or less as it had done the previous day when he, Ed and Clarissa had taken their leave. All the trays and dishes were piled up ready for Monday, while only a handful of cakes, bakes, biscuits and buns remained—presumably for decoration as they'd be too stale to sell come the morning.

Toby made his way behind the counter. There were shelves containing takeaway cups and lids, stirrers, sugar, paper serviettes, paper bags, ribbon, scissors, order pads, till rolls, a calculator, a stapler, pens, a couple of catalogues and so on and so forth.

"Stuff that's useful, I suppose." Toby sniffed everything but, mindful of what Clarissa had been saying, decided it would be better not to lick or otherwise touch anything. This also meant not moving anything to look behind it. "Severely limiting," Toby muttered.

He sniffed around the door frame before standing and staring out through the glass at people passing. He could see everyone, and clearly they could see him because a few hoomans smiled to see him there, and a scruffy lurcher had the temerity to bark at him.

"Excuse you!" Toby barked back. "I have every right to be—huh!" He caught his breath and raised his snout to stare at the ceiling. Clarissa and Dee Dee were somewhere above his head. If Clarissa heard him, she'd be straight down here to give him an earbashing.

He glared at the lurcher until it finally walked away. *I'll see you another time*, Toby telegraphed.

Satisfied he'd won that battle, he examined the floor beneath the tables. This was an easy task because the chairs had been placed on the tables and the floor swept and washed.

"I don't know what I expected to find, but I didn't find it," Toby remarked, trotting back through the internal door and waving a paw at the door into the next room. The lock clicked, the handle turned and he entered more cautiously than before.

Dark.

Shadowy.

There might be monsters ...

"*Illuminate*!" he announced, and the lights flicked on, dull at first but rapidly becoming brighter.

This was the bakery proper. The place where the magick happened. There was a pair of sparkling silver ovens, evidently brand new, pushed against the wall, with an enormous elephant's trunk hanging above them. *A vent,* Toby decided. *Or an escape hatch for witches and wizards who need to get away in a hurry.*

It was impossible to tell. "Worth considering," Toby said, noting the clue.

There was also the biggest fridge Toby had ever seen. It had a pair of wide doors. His heart beat a merry little salsa as he magicked one of them open. He was disappointed to find tall piles of butter and plastic storage trays full of different chocolates and fruits.

"You could definitely keep a body in there," Toby decided.

In the centre of the space was a massive preparation table. Beneath it were shelves with scores of baking trays and cake pans, and muffin trays and rolling pins and jelly moulds and mixing bowls and more cake pans and ... things Toby had never seen before so he couldn't put a name to. He inched around the table, sniffing everything but once again careful not to disturb anything.

On a side counter he could see—by stretching up on his back legs—mixing machines. Big ones. And a fryer. And a sink. *You could barf a dog or two in that,* he thought and backed away, just in case he somehow managed to fall in even though it was over three feet above the floor.

You can never be too careful.

On higher shelves were bags and sacks containing specialist sugars and flours and cocoas and herbs and spices. There were jars containing glittery things and multicoloured things and decorations and sparkling liquids in rainbow colours. There were toppers and muffin cases and piles of napkins wrapped in plastic. There were jars full of silicone spatulas and mixing implements, and even a box labelled 'fireworks'.

Ooo-er! Toby backed off. "Why would you keep bombs in your bakery?" he wondered aloud. "Highly suspicious if you ask me."

But that was it.

Apart from the tall plastic barrels by the rear door. These were marked alternately as flour and sugar. He came closer and inhaled. *Hmmm.* If you were going to hide poison, this would be a good starting point. You could mix some powdered forms of poisons into one of these barrels and no-one would ever know, would they?

The problem was, he couldn't tell either. He would have to disturb the barrels and remove the lids in order to take a close sniff and, while he wasn't averse to doing that, if Clarissa caught him, she'd be sure to try to rehome him.

And that would never do.

He backtracked, unsure what else to take a closer look at. Everything smelled clean and fresh and newly painted, and these scents dominated all others, perhaps with the notable exceptions of chocolate and vanilla. If Toby had been a perfumier, these were the only scents he would have tried to sell to his customers.

Or maybe a little Eau de Badger Poop.

Or a cheeky little fragrance named Salty Sunrise and Spoiled Seagull Corpse.

Or ...

A scuffling sound from the very corner of the bakery alerted Toby to a newcomer. His head swivelled quickly and he scanned to his right, catching sight of whiskers in a gap between the fridge and the wall.

"Hey!" he called. "Come out, come out. WPDCD Silverwind here with a search warrant."

He didn't have a warrant, of course, but the bewhiskered gentleman or lady was not to know that.

The whiskers twitched.

"Come on out, or I'll send the dogs in!" Toby called.

The whiskers paused for a long second before a furry face emerged to take a better look. "You are the dogs," it said.

"That's true," Toby replied. "Well observed. I'm WP—"

"I know who you is, matey. I heard you the first time. But I don't care."

Toby sat down, a little taken aback by the fact that his authority was being called into question. "That's not the right attitude."

"It's the only attitude you're going to get from me, barky-boy. Buzz off."

"I'd like to ask you a few questions—"

The rat glared out at Toby with angry black eyes. "And I'd like not to supply you with any answers. Now do one, fuzzy face!" With that final admonishment, the rat withdrew its head from view and disappeared.

That told me!

Footsteps ... Toby crooked his head. Outside. Someone was approaching the rear of the property. He could clearly hear voices through the battered external door a matter of feet from where he was sitting.

"Upstairs, I expect," a woman said.

"What about this door? Do you think this is the back entrance to the shop?" A male voice.

"A storeroom?" the woman queried. "I'll go up. You stay here a minute."

Uh-oh. Police! Toby decided. *They'll be knocking on the door any minute. Maybe the chap will kick in the door here! Time to make myself scarce.* "Nice to meet you," he called out to the rat. He preferred to leave things in good standing. He hurried up the stairs, managed to get halfway before realising he hadn't closed the door, and scrambled back down.

"*Clauditis*!" he ordered, and the door closed and locked itself. He was panting by the time he made it back up to the flat. The knock came almost immediately. He sidled into the kitchen and threw himself onto the floor, pretending to be asleep as Dee Dee walked past to answer the door.

"Hello," Dee Dee said. She sounded a little calmer than she had earlier. Clarissa's distraction techniques had obviously been working.

"Dee Dee Adamus?" the woman's voice asked. "DC Flanagan from Sun Valley Police. I wondered if I'd be able to ask you a few questions?"

"What's it regarding?" Dee Dee asked, her voice steady. Toby decided now was a good time to put in an appearance. He trotted out of the kitchen and joined Dee Dee at the door.

"It's regarding a sudden death that we're looking into. Would it be alright for my colleague and I to come in?" DC Flanagan dropped her gaze to study Toby warily.

He offered her his best smile. "WPDCD Silverwind," he told her. "We're on the same side."

"Toby?" The tones in Clarissa's voice, from the direction of the living area, were laden with disapproval, warning, fondness *and* threat. How did she manage to do that?

"Yes, come in," said Dee Dee. There wasn't much else she could say to a request from the police to ask her a few—as far as she was aware—innocuous questions. "Don't mind Toby," she said, stepping back to allow the detective to enter. "He's completely harmless."

CHAPTER SEVEN

"I fail to understand why you took umbrage at that," Moriarty said later.

She, Sal and Toby were sitting on the roof of Toby's wizarding shed, having indulged in a little gossip during the Twilight Barking. There wasn't a huge amount happening around Sun Valley this evening. An old Border collie had passed away on Sweet Down Farm, just out of town on the road to Lyme Regis, and folk were sharing their memories of her attending country fairs and riding in the back of her dad's pickup on their frequent forays into town and to the supermarket, but that was about it.

Oh, and a Pekingese had eaten a pair of his mum's red lacy underpants and had to be taken to the vet to endure a procedure that had cost A LOT

OF MONEY. But apart from that, and a reminder that the pet shop on Mayflower Lane would be open in the morning—it closed on Sundays, too—there wasn't much for anyone to report.

Since the proceedings had finished early, Toby had been sharing his day's experiences with his rapt audience. That is, he liked to think they were fascinated by all he was saying, but Moriarty was washing her ears and Sal was busy gnawing on a bone he'd found in number twelve's open bin, and Toby couldn't be sure either was fully absorbed in his stories.

Despite Moriarty's deliberate and thorough grooming ritual, at least she was engaged enough with what he was saying to ask intelligent and pertinent questions when Toby paused to breathe or think.

"I took umbrage because I'm not harmless. I am a fierce warrior dog," Toby reminded her.

Moriarty delicately licked her paw. "You really aren't."

"Why does everyone think I'm cute and fluffy?" Toby couldn't hide his outrage.

"Because you're one of the sweetest dogs I know," Moriarty explained. "There's not a bad bone in your body."

Sal jumped, recognising some of the words Moriarty had spoken. "You can't have it." He clamped his skinny little arms around the bone he'd been nibbling on.

Moriarty's bright green eyes settled on him in a most unnerving way. Toby slid between them. He sometimes worried that Moriarty would pounce on Sal one day and put an end to him. This was one reason he liked to share as many treats as possible with her, to make sure she was never hungry enough to act on impulse.

"We weren't talking about your wretched bone," Moriarty purred, leaning sideways so she could catch a glimpse of Sal. "We were talking about Toby's."

"My bones aren't wretched!" Toby inserted, his eyebrows knitting together.

"So what happened after that?" Moriarty didn't take back her comment about his wretched bones or the one accusing him of being sweet. Toby had a feeling she was in a bad mood, but it was difficult to tell because, being a cat, she didn't like to show much emotion. You would never accuse Moriarty of wearing her heart on her sleeve, that was for sure.

"Clarissa made me sit right next to her while the police came in and asked Dee Dee some questions." Toby thought back to the interview. Dee Dee hadn't been arrested. Nothing like that. The detectives appeared to be on a fact-finding mission. They didn't confirm the mayor had died from poisoning, but they did allude to it.

"Would it be alright if I took a little look around?" the male detective had asked, and again Dee Dee had consented.

"I have nothing to hide," she'd told them. "What exactly are you looking for?"

"One of the possibilities we're exploring is that the mayor died from something he came into contact with yesterday. Either something he ate or drank or something he inhaled, or perhaps something that was sprayed onto his skin." The female detective had stared fixedly at Dee Dee as her colleague had donned a pair of blue plastic gloves and wandered off towards the kitchen.

Dee Dee had squirmed in her chair. "Obviously you already know that Mayor Casterford attended the opening of my bakery yesterday."

DC Flanagan had nodded. "We checked his appointments with his office. Did he eat anything while he was here?"

"I should think so," Dee Dee had answered. "There were trays and plates of baked goods I'd prepared especially for the occasion." She looked in the direction of the kitchen, where the other DC was pulling drawers and cabinet doors open.

"Like a buffet?"

"Exactly. A baked goods buffet. A sample of many of the items that will be on the menu at The Magick Muffin." She'd sounded proud.

"Did you see the mayor eat anything?"

Dee Dee had paused here, casting her mind back. She'd frowned. "I don't recall. I was run off my feet. There were lots of people here. More than I'd expected."

The male DC had popped his head around the corner. "Is it alright if I have a look downstairs?"

"Yes. Let me get you the keys—" Dee Dee had stood, found her handbag and rummaged inside until she came across them. She'd handed them over. "They're the two old keys, there."

"Thank you."

Toby had spoken up. "I wouldn't bother trying to interview the rat. He doesn't like detectives."

Clarissa had reached down and gently clamped his snout closed. "Sssh!"

"Did you know everyone who attended yesterday?" DC Flanagan had continued asking her questions as her partner clunked his way downstairs, eyeballing Toby once more.

"No, not at all. I haven't lived here in Sun Valley for long. I know a few people and I'm getting to know others." Dee Dee had indicated Clarissa, who squeezed her hand.

"Why Sun Valley?" Flanagan had asked.

Dee Dee had shrugged. "It's such a lovely place. Wonderful people. Gorgeous surroundings. A relatively small community that I feel I can be a part of. And people who enjoy baked goods. That was an important consideration, given what I'm trying to sell."

"And had you had much to do with the mayor before yesterday?"

"Not a great amount, no. We'd spoken briefly on the phone."

"I'm curious about how you managed to get him to agree to open the bakery," Flanagan had said. "Did you pay him? I mean if you didn't know him and hadn't had much to do with him. Because he can sometimes be reticent to, erm ..." Her voice trailed off.

Clarissa had picked up the thread. "Do things for free," she'd finished for the detective. "Mayor Casterford is known for being a tad stingy. He has a reputation for only doing things for 'donations' and under-the-table backhanders—"

"It sounds like you have a beef with the mayor," the detective had said, arching an eyebrow.

Clarissa had held her hands up. "Not at all. I'm only repeating what I've heard. There are lots of rumours about Mayor Casterford. I'm sure you've heard plenty."

The detective hadn't commented on that, but her lips had curled up slightly at the edges.

"And that was it," Toby finished as Moriarty cleaned her left ear and Sal pushed his bone away, his jaw probably aching from the endless gnawing.

"Did the man detective find anything?" Moriarty asked.

"I don't think so." Toby hadn't seen him carrying anything when he climbed back up the stairs. "But he did tell Dee Dee not to touch anything until their inquiries were completed. She wasn't happy about that. She was supposed to be opening normally tomorrow."

"And the rat didn't tell him anything, I suppose?" Sal asked. He had been listening after all.

"Don't be ridiculous," scoffed Moriarty. "Hoomans don't speak rat."

"Maybe rats choose not to speak to hoomans, think about that," said Sal.

"That particular rat didn't want to speak to

anyone," Toby noted. "The most insulting and unfriendly creature I've ever come across."

"And you've met a fair few of them," Sal said and smiled at Moriarty.

Moriarty ignored the dig. "Presumably rats speak to rats?" she asked.

"Depends wevver they've got anythin' interesting to say," said Sal, taking a renewed interest in the bone that was now so devoid of flesh and cartilage that it was beginning to shine as the moon rose above the horizon.

Toby observed Moriarty with delight. "I see where you're going with that."

"With what?" Something in Toby's voice made Sal look up.

Toby chortled. "With you, as it turns out. I think you and I are going to take a little walk into town to The Magick Muffin."

"Huh?" Sal clutched at his bone again. "I'm busy! Can't you see that?"

"I would be happy to accompany you." Moriarty's eyes sparkled. "I take an interest in all things rodent."

"Whaaaaaat?" Sal paled. He pointed at Toby and then at Moriarty. "I ain't goin' nowhere if—"

"It's fine, it's fine!" Toby hurried to intercede. He

nodded at Moriarty. "Thanks for the offer and, erm ... thanks for the brilliant idea, but we'll take it from here."

"Of course." Moriarty bowed her head, blinked once, then turned and elegantly leapt from the top of the shed to land on the fence. Before Toby could say goodbye, she'd disappeared into Mrs Crouch's hedge.

"Gee." Sal sounded disgruntled.

Toby nudged him. "I guess if we're going on a detecting mission, I'm going to have to recruit you to my detective agency."

Sal perked up at this. "When do I get paid?"

"There's no remuneration," Toby told him, "only a status." He lowered himself down so Sal could grab hold of his collar. "So, I'm the lead detective. The WPDCD–kind of like a high sheriff, right?" Lately Toby and Sal had been enjoying some black and white westerns on afternoon telly.

"Right," said Sal.

"And you can be my second in command!"

"There's only two of us," Sal reminded him.

"For now! Climb aboard, Deputy Salvatore Messio!"

"Deputy?" Sal fluffed himself up to his full fat furry ball self. "Cor!"

"Hang on tight." Toby manoeuvred his way

down the ladder stairs. “Let’s go and do some detecting.”

“Yeeha!” Sal sang as Toby—at pace—began to navigate his way out of their garden. “Deputy Sal! Cor!”

Moriarty had found her way to the gatepost. She gazed down at them as they hurried past.

“Go get ’em, cowboys,” she said, chuckling to herself.

CHAPTER EIGHT

Toby hated to do it, but the only way he could see they could gain access to the bakery was to go through the rear external door. It wasn't ideal, but a much better option than trying to go through the front door from the shop itself and thereby risk being noticed, or trying to go in through the apartment door.

Toby didn't want to alert Dee Dee to what he was doing.

Lights glinted from the windows upstairs, which meant Dee Dee was home. "We need to be as quiet as mice," Toby told Sal as the rat slid off his back.

"Mice ain't that quiet," Sal told him. "Have you seen how big their families get? You try keeping a household full of baby mice occupied. You think rats are bad, but—"

"Sssh!" Toby hissed. It wasn't that he was afraid of Dee Dee hearing Sal, so much as Sal drawing unwanted attention from other animals in the proximity. Cats with an appetite, owls even ... perhaps other dogs. Toby didn't want a barking match.

He'd win, but that wasn't the point.

He also needed to concentrate on opening the door. It wasn't particularly complicated. The locks were old and easy enough to disable, but their age made them altogether creakier. Of late, he'd spent a decent amount of time learning how to unlock and lock things, open stuff, close it and make sure it was secure. Something about his experiences with The Pointy Woman had made him aware of how much life can change in a split second. He wanted to be able to get himself out of any situation in which he found himself hemmed in as quickly and efficiently as possible. Fortunately, with the aid of Rory's grimoire—a remarkable read—and some additional training from Dominic Lavery, the chaos wizard, on his infrequent visits to Honeystick Farm, he'd been making good progress.

So now he gazed up at the door and began to imagine the inside layout of the locks. Whether the locks looked anything like the images he could conjure up is debatable. But that's not what magick is about. Toby pulled together pictures of rods and tumblers, springs and coils, sprockets and cogs, and when he had them clearly at the forefront of his mind, he imagined coating them all with oil, working through the nooks, the crannies and the teeth, then, when everything was slick and slippery, Toby evaporated everything in its entirety and imagined a dark void there instead.

Click.

The door, until now uptight and secure, visibly relaxed.

Toby nodded, satisfied. "Let's go," he whispered, and the pair of them slipped through the gap into the bakery, pushing the door to behind them but not fully closing it, just in case they needed to make a rapid getaway.

"*Illuminate!*" Toby ordered, and the lights blinked on. He lifted his head to study the fluorescent strips. They were the kind of lights that were dull at first but rapidly grew brighter as they warmed up. Toby didn't want that—the light would be seen through the crack in the door, or Dee Dee might spot it spilling out down the bottom of the stairs. "*Mute!*" he said, and the lights cooled down so that the bakery became shadowy but not completely dark.

Sal stopped by the preparation table, his whiskers working overtime. "Cor!" he said. "Lots of nice smells in here." He hurried over to the fridge. "There's cheese in 'ere!" he announced. "Any chance you could open this up for me, Toby?"

"Absolutely not," Toby whispered. "We're on the right side of the law! We're not a pair of thieves. Remember?"

"Oh, yeah, yeah. I was forgettin'. You're right." Sal smoothed his fur down. "I'm a deputy. An enforcerer of law and orderer. No. An enforcerer of lawer ... no—"

"Here!" Toby indicated the side of the fridge. "Your mate's down there."

Sal scurried over to Toby's side and peered along the gap between the fridge and the wall. "He's not my mate."

"You shared a pocket with him," said Toby.

"We didn't get intimately acquainted." Sal sounded most put out.

"You shared Ed's breast pocket. That means you're bosom buddies." Toby chuckled at his own joke.

"I deny everything!" Sal squeaked. "I only have

eyes for my one and only." He meant Hedda, a hedgehog they'd met on their previous adventure. They were an odd couple, but it seemed to work for them.

Toby nodded down the gap. "See if you can get your ma—I mean, this other rat *of our acquaintance* to come out and chat."

Sal stuck his bottom lip out. "He probably won't."

"Give it a try ... Deputy," Toby said.

That seemed to do the trick. Sal edged along the side of the fridge, his back to the wall, until he was about halfway down. Clearing his throat, he called, "Hello? Hello?" When there was no response, he tried again, lowering the timbre of his voice to sound more official. "Good evening? It's the, erm—" He glanced back at Toby, unsure what they were. Toby had explained the WD wotsit thingie, but Sal had forgotten what it meant. And then he'd been made a deputy, which surely made Toby a sheriff, so Toby was a sheriff *and* a wizard *and* a private detective, which—now that Sal tried to unpick it all—seemed incredibly confusing.

Toby nodded his encouragement, mistaking Sal's glance back at him as a need for reassurance.

"—It's the erm ... sheriff's police department,

wizarding division," Sal called, sensing Toby's surprise without turning round.

"Is it?" asked a scathing voice. "Is it *really*?" The voice didn't come from behind the fridge or indeed anywhere in the vicinity. It came from somewhere behind them.

"Ow!" Toby yelped in surprise. A moment later something clattered on the floor.

Sal spun round.

"Hey!" Toby yelped again, albeit as quietly as he could manage. There was a ping and a clang.

"What's happening?" Sal asked, afraid to come out from the side of the fridge.

"We're being attacked by hostiles! Take cover!" Toby ordered, entirely unnecessarily given that Sal had yet to *break* cover. "We're being pinned down by enemy insurgents. Mayday! Mayday!" Toby had no radio and there was no-one to communicate with, but he'd seen enough war films to understand that regardless of whether you thought anyone could hear you or not, you had to keep trying. You never knew when the cavalry might arrive!

For his part, Toby dived onto the shelf under the table, knocking baking trays and mixing bowls and cake pans in all directions, conducting a short but alarming and surreal orchestration of clangs and dings and clunks. As it came to an end, silence fell. Toby, under the table, gazed heavenwards, unable to see anything except the underside of some drawers but trying to imagine where the attacker was. And Dee Dee? Whereabouts upstairs was she? Had she heard the noise? Was she on her way down? Did he need to evacuate?

Holding his breath, he cocked his head, first one way then another. His ears twitched and flapped. He couldn't sense any movement.

"Sal?" he whispered.

Sal, eyes wide, poked his head out from the shadows. "All present and correct, Sheriff."

Something whizzed through the air from somewhere above Toby's head and struck Sal right between the eyes. Sal keeled over, paws up.

Oh boy! Rat down! Toby eased his way forward, trying not to upset any more pots and pans. "Sal?" he hissed. "Sal?"

Without a response, Toby began to panic. *Oh no! What have I done?* His heart fluttered. *I should have known better than to come here without backup! If I'd brought reinforcements, this might not have happened.* "Sal?"

When all remained quiet and Sal still didn't

move, Toby had no choice. He had to get out from beneath the table and drag the rat to safety.

Toby inched forward, ears flat against his head, eyes swivelling as he tried to look everywhere at once. Once his paws were back on the tiles, he scurried forward, observed Sal on his back, paws in the air and tongue out and grabbed the rat by his tail.

"Hey!" Sal sat up. "Watch what you're doing! It won't grow back, y'kno—"

Another missile soared past Toby's head and bounced off the fridge, hitting him on the cheek as it rebounded. Toby jerked his head back, but it hadn't hurt him. It was more the shock than anything. The acceleration had gone out of whatever it was, and it dropped beside him. Ignoring it, he spun around, blocking Sal from any more flying objects.

Movement. There! On top of the table.

"Oi!" Toby shouted, before remembering Dee Dee might hear him bark. A slight figure peered out from behind a jar, a missile in its paw.

A rat!

The rat!

"Hey!" Toby snapped. "Do not throw that. Do not—"

The rat danced forward and swung its teeny

paw. The light-coloured object flew through the air and, with deadly accuracy, hit Toby on the snout.

He blinked.

"It's chocolate!" Sal called.

"What?" Toby half turned to Sal as the other rat pelted him again, this time with a dark-coloured pellet.

"Chocolate!" Sal danced in ecstasy. "It's raining chocolate buttons!"

"Are you sure?" Toby scoured the tiles for one and sniffed it suspiciously. It smelt sweet and vanilla-y. Mmm. He was about to scoop it up with his happy tongue when he remembered that the reason he was here in the first place was because someone had been *poisoned*—and they might have been poisoned in this very bakery. His tongue froze where it was. "Uuugggh."

"What's the matter?" Sal asked, salsa-ing out into the open and shaking his shoulders, paws outstretched, an open invitation to the other rat to keep throwing the buttons. "Over 'ere, son! On me 'ead."

The other rat obliged, clipping Sal's ear.

Sal roared with maniacal laughter.

"It's poison," said Toby.

"Hahahahaha! You what?" Sal asked, reaching for another button.

"Don't eat them! They're poison!"

The mirth deserted Sal in one exhalation. "They can't be poison. I've already eaten half a dozen."

A dark chocolate button smacked Sal's shoulder. He wafted at where it had been, his excitement deflated.

"Will you stop throwing things?" Toby growled at the other rat.

"Yeah!" Sal had turned pale. "It's getting annoying now."

"How are you feeling?" Toby asked, studying Sal's complexion for signs that he was dying. This wasn't easy given that Toby didn't know what to look for in a poison victim, and also because Sal was a rat and therefore had a furry face, but the pinks of his eyes—and his lips and paws—were always pale. Still, he was definitely looking a little sallow.

"A bit strange," Sal admitted.

"That might just be from eating too much chocolate," Toby suggested. "Clarissa tells me that chocolate is poisonous for dogs."

"Even without poison in?" Sal asked, wafting his face.

"Apparently."

Sal blew out his cheeks. "So this might be poisonous poisonous? Twice as deadly?"

"It may well be ... but ..." Toby crouched down all the better to see Sal's face. "If it was doubly poisonous ... wouldn't something have happened by now?"

They stood staring at each other, waiting for some reaction, as chocolate buttons rained down from above until eventually, the shower of sweets stopped. Sal took a deep breath and shrugged hard.

"Nope," he said. "I'm still alive!"

"Hey!" the other rat shouted down. "What are you geezers doing?"

Toby shot a fierce look his way. "Are you trying to poison us?" he asked. *Might as well be direct about it.*

The rat wrinkled his nose. "No, I'm trying to stone yous to death, obviously."

"You'll have to find something a bit more substantial than chocolate buttons if you want to do that," said Toby. "And anyway, just pack it in. We're—"

"Oh, here it comes." The bakery rat rolled his eyes. "More nonsense about being the police—"

"Not the police," Toby clarified. "We're detectives. *Private* detectives."

"Yeah, and I'm a troll in the Hall of the Mountain King."

Toby and Sal exchanged glances. They weren't sure who the Mountain King was, but he sounded important.

"I ... er ... well, we're pleased to meet you and perhaps you could send felicitations to your ... erm ... to His Majesty," Toby said.

The bakery rat snorted. "Yeah. I'll send 'em. Whatever fliss-ti-taytos are."

"I dunno either," said Sal. "But I'd like to try 'em."

"We'd like to ask you some questions," Toby tried again. He was a trying kind of dog.

"I've told you before, I don't want nothin' to do with you or your questions. I have no interest in your questions. Whatever yous want, it has nothin' to do with me, alright?"

"It will only take a few minutes," Toby pleaded. "And then we'll be out of your fur furever."

"You ain't hearing me, are you?" The bakery rat leaned over and hoisted something off the top of the table. It caught the light as the rat raised it above his head. A millisecond later, whatever it was came flying through the air, tip over tail, until it zinged in front of Toby's snout and stuck into the floor.

Toby glanced down and squealed. The rat had thrown a two-pronged carving fork at him, and the tines had impaled themselves into the floor on either side of his right paw.

"Wow," said Sal, impressed by the bakery rat's throwing skills. "Such accuracy!"

Toby swallowed. He might have ended up toeless!

"Accurate?" the bakery rat screeched. "I missed!"

Toby began to inch away. This rotten rodent was a total bad'n. And bonkers with it!

"But I won't miss next time!" The bakery rat hoisted a carving knife above his head.

That was enough for Toby. "Let's get out of here," he said, ducking as the knife whizzed past him, far too close for comfort, and embedded itself in the stainless steel door of the fridge.

Above their heads, the ceiling creaked. Dee Dee had finally noticed the disturbance. Toby scooped up Sal by the scruff of his neck and made a break for the door. Behind them the bakery rat laughed crazily, but by the time Dee Dee unlocked the internal door and stepped into the bakery, the external door had been closed and secured and there wasn't a creature in sight ...

"What in the world?" Dee Dee asked.

She frowned at the pots, pans and mixing implements that littered the floor and recoiled at the knife embedded in the fridge door, still quivering. But most peculiar of all were the chocolate buttons scattered over the top of her preparation table and randomly yet purposefully distributed across the tiled floor.

CHAPTER NINE

Toby jumped through the dog flap and inspected his bowl. Empty.

Again.

"Always empty," he muttered.

"That's because you empty it," Clarissa called from the living room.

Ears of a bat, thought Toby.

"I don't remember having my dinner," Toby said, trotting into the living room to see what Clarissa was up to.

She was sitting at the dining room table staring at her computer screen.

"Just because you don't remember, doesn't mean it didn't happen." Clarissa pursed her lips, although not at Toby. She was glowering at whatever was on the screen. "Fortunately, I remember serving it to you, so we're not both becoming old and senile." She turned her head and smiled, reaching out to offer him a scritch.

Tony gave the scritch a moment's consideration before deciding to give in and accept it. He climbed onto the chair beside Clarissa and allowed her to fuss him.

"Where have you been?" she asked.

"Out for a wander," Toby answered vaguely. That was kind of true.

She leaned over to kiss the soft fur between his ears. "Oooh, you smell sweet—"

"What are you doing?" Toby quickly interrupted her before she could figure out what he'd been up to. Clarissa wasn't daft. Give her an inch ... He trod on her thigh and headbutted her chin for good measure.

"Ow!" Clarissa pushed him off. "Ooh!" She massaged her thigh. "You're a great gallumphing idiot sometimes!"

"But you love me," sang Toby, grateful his plan had worked. "Are you writing about Dee Dee's case?"

"Not exactly," said Clarissa. "Well, kind of, maybe."

"That cleared that up," Toby said, widening his eyes.

"I'm looking at photos." Clarissa pointed at her laptop. "I've uploaded all the ones I took yesterday."

Toby leaned closer to get a better look. The one currently occupying the screen had been taken outside The Magick Muffin. The mayor was making his speech, looking simultaneously crumpled and disgruntled. There were members of the crowd at the edges of the shot, and Dee Dee could be seen holding a tray of cake samples towards a woman with pale-blue curly hair—quite old-fashioned despite not really looking that old—and wearing a purple paisley dress.

"Are you hoping you caught whoever poisoned the mayor on film?" Toby asked. That would be quite a coup!

"If only it could be that easy, eh?"

"I remember her," Toby said, indicating the woman in the dress.

"Do you? I never noticed her." Clarissa lay her head to one side. "I don't recognise her."

"There's no way you'd recognise everyone in town," said Toby, although he had a feeling *he* knew of every dog within a five-mile radius.

"No. I suppose not." Clarissa flicked to the next

photo. A lovely one of Dee Dee brandishing a tray of goodies. This one made Toby feel hungry again. "I really don't see how Dee Dee could have poisoned one person out of a whole horde of folks who sampled her cakes and bakes yesterday. There were dozens of us."

"Maybe other people haven't come forward yet," Toby suggested.

"But I'm not sick. You're not sick." Clarissa thought for a moment. "I'm pretty sure if Ed was sick —and, let's face it, given the size of that muffin he polished off, he deserves to be—I'd have known about it long before now."

"He'd want nursing," Toby agreed.

"He'd want the whole world to be aware of just how ill he was," Clarissa added.

"Of course, if other people had become as sick as the mayor, they might all be lying in their beds, dead as doornails."

"Eww. Toby—"

"Waiting to be discovered—"

"Toby!" Clarissa grimaced. "You have an awful imagination sometimes. I'm sure they'd have been found by now."

"Not if they don't have loved ones. Lots of people live on their own."

"You're horrible." Clarissa leaned away from him.

"Maybe the police need to employ cadaver dogs. You know ... we can smell death—"

Clarissa erupted. "Toby!"

Toby took the hint. "Alright. Alright."

He remained quiet for a while as Clarissa clicked through and studied each image until eventually a photo of him and Ed came up. They were gazing at each other. Toby was standing on Ed's boot.

"So cute!" Clarissa stroked the screen.

"I know I am," Toby preened.

"I meant Ed," said Clarissa, and giggled.

"Hmpf!" Toby was just about to complain when Clarissa's phone made a *beeby-de-beep* sound. She picked it up and activated it.

"A WhatsApp from Dee Dee," she said. "Oh." The phone *beebeedeebeeped* again. And again. Then a couple of photos came through. "That's odd." Clarissa turned the phone to show Toby the disarray in the bakery. "She's thinking she had a break-in. Mess everywhere."

"Really?" Toby asked. "Oh dear."

Beeby-de-beep.

"Chocolate buttons all over the floor." Clarissa

narrowed her eyes and swivelled in her chair. "Where did you say you were tonight?"

Toby yawned, widening his mouth in exaggeration and then shaking his head. "Oooh. I'm done in."

"Toby?"

"Is that the time?" Toby hadn't even looked at the time. He jumped down from his chair. "Think I'll head outside for a garden check and then turn in." He began inching towards the kitchen.

"Toby!"

"Sleep tight! See you in the morning!" With that, he leapt through the dog flap and dashed up the garden to seek refuge out of sight under a bush. He hunkered down, watching the back door in case Clarissa followed him. She didn't.

"Obvs I'm not staying out here all night," Toby said, watching the lights in the house. He'd know when Clarissa went to bed.

"Are you talking to yourself?" Sal picked that moment to pass by, clutching a tomato in each hand. Presumably he'd been robbing someone's garden. Clarissa didn't grow tomatoes, but the old chap who lived behind them did.

"I'm talking to the most interesting and intelligent dog I know," Toby confirmed.

"Uh-huh."

"And trying to escape the wrath of Clarissa, who suspects us of breaking and entering The Magick Muffin. The absolute cheek of the woman!"

"To be fair, we did do that," Sal said, taking a bite of one of his tomatoes. "Cor. Jooooooooceeeee!"

"That's beside the point," said Toby, who had often heard Clarissa repeat this phrase and thought it was quite a clever saying. *Beside* the point. Not *the* point, but *close*. Extremely close. "Are you going to eat both of those tomatoes?"

Sal stopped munching, juice dribbling down his chin. "I was going to," he said, his mouth full. "Why?"

"Sharing is caring."

"You don't like tomatoes."

"That's not the point either."

Sal sighed and held out a whole tomato. Toby sniffed it and wrinkled his nose.

"I knew it!" said Sal and disposed of his half-eaten one in one giant mouthful before starting on the next one.

"I'm hungry," Toby complained. "Apparently I had my dinner, but it was so long ago I can't remember it."

"I'm sure we still have some treats in the tin in the shed," Sal said.

We? Toby decided to overlook that for the time being. "Oh? I thought we'd finished them? I was meaning to visit Mrs Crouch and ... erm ... surreptitiously ... hint at the need to restock. Let's have a look."

They skipped along to the shed together, Sal's little legs having to move faster than Toby's. Once inside, Toby levitated the old Quality Street tin down from the shelf and removed the lid. His ability to control objects was improving all the time. Recently he'd been successful at levitating the kettle. It didn't have any water in at the time, but that was the next step.

As they shared the treats out—not quite equally, seeing as Toby was about twenty times the size and volume of Sal, despite Sal being a heavyweight rodent—Toby considered the events of the evening. As Sal tucked into one of the fishy treats Mrs Crouch had supplied them with, Toby realised the rat's appetite was as hearty as ever.

"Clearly you weren't poisoned," Toby said.

"Huh?" Sal paused mid-chew.

"The chocolate buttons."

Sal shrugged. "Maybe chocolate isn't poisonous to rats."

"But it wasn't poisonous poisonous either, otherwise you'd be dead."

"True." Sal patted his tummy. "I should have eaten more of them."

"Everyone seems to be assuming—" Toby wiggled his head. *Everyone* was a generalisation, seeing as he wasn't sure anyone was assuming anything except him ... "that Dee Dee poisoned the mayor with a cake or a sausage roll or something, right?"

"Mmm?" Sal carried on nibbling.

"But she would have had to poison everyone in order to target him, unless she managed to give him something that nobody else ate."

"She tried to give him a box of treats to take home," Sal reminded him.

Toby had forgotten about that. "But he refused them."

"I wonder what happened to them," Sal said, thinking what a treat it would be to discover a box of cakes going begging.

"Mmm." Toby thought some thoughts. "She would have to have cornered the mayor by himself later ..."

"By visiting him at home?" Sal asked.

"Yes. I wonder if the detectives have checked out

her movements from last night." Toby was certain they would have done if they were seriously suspecting Dee Dee. It's the sort of thing they always did on the television shows that Toby liked to watch. There would be CCTV and doorbell cameras and all that kind of malarkey.

"Plus you guys are all pre-supposin' that Dee Dee has a motive for wanting the mayor out of the way," Sal said, reaching for a cheesy treat. He knew these were Toby's favourite favourites, so he was pushing his luck here.

Toby watched Sal carefully. "We were there. Me, you, Clarissa, Ed. We all heard what she said. Ed thought that was important enough to drop by and warn her about an impending investigation."

"I know," Sal said, holding out the cheesy treat. He didn't want to run the risk of being kicked out of the shed tonight. The weather was set to be changeable over the next few days, according to the barometer that Toby's friend—and ex-zombie—Old Pete had attached to the outside wall of the shed. "What I'm saying is, he was a bit of a meanie, weren't he? He didn't like rats. He was quite threat'nin' ... In my experience, folk like that have previous."

"Previous? Previous what?"

"Previous meanness. You don't get to be that mean without practice, right?"

Finally, Toby cottoned on to what Sal was saying. "He'll have other enemies? That's true. I'm sure the police will investigate that angle too." Maybe he'd run that by Ed the next time he saw him —with a little help from Clarissa translating—just in case Ed hadn't considered it. Perhaps he and Sal could stake out the town council's offices and see what people who worked there thought of him. He reached out to accept the treat from Sal.

As he was about to pop the cheesy titbit—mmm, it smelled soooooo good—into his mouth and demolish it with one ferocious bite, Sal raised a pink finger. "And Dee Dee too, of course."

"Dee Dee what?" Toby fumbled the treat and it rolled under the bookcase. *Blast!*

"Dee Dee will have enemies too."

"She's only just moved here. She doesn't know anyone," Toby argued.

"Ha! She doesn't need to know anyone, does she? Other people know her. Or at least *of* her and her bakery."

"Seems like a long shot," Toby replied, but doubting himself. Sal was right. She might already have enemies.

"You're probably right," said Sal. "You're the sheriff. I'm only the deputy. Shall I rescue that runaway delectable for you?"

"Thanks." Toby watched as Sal squirmed his cuddly butt underneath the bottom shelf and fished around for the treat. Thinking aloud, he said, "But yes, you could be right ... It's a different angle. A different way to look at it."

"That's what I was thinking." Sal's voice was muffled. A moment later he reappeared, triumphantly waving the treat. Dust and fluff flew in all directions. Sal sneezed. "'Ere ya go, guv'nor."

Toby pulled a face. "You have it," he said. "I think I'm going to go inside and up to bed."

"Very gracious of ya," Sal said, brushing off the worst of the fluff.

"Food for thought," Toby said as he backed out of the shed. "Goodnight."

"Night!" Sal carried his treat over to his shredded basket and settled in. "Food for thought," he repeated, and stuffed the whole treat in his gob at once.

CHAPTER TEN

"I'm looking into it, but so far there really isn't enough for me to write up," Clarissa was saying. The boss had phoned again this morning, although thankfully not as early as the day before. At least this time Clarissa was up and showered. Toby, meanwhile, was on the hunt for second breakfast, having wolfed down the first.

"No, I don't think Dee Dee did it," Clarissa said, sounding annoyed and a little defensive. "Because she's my friend and she's one of us. If she wanted to kill Mayor Casterford she could have done it far more easily than with poison, and she'd have left no trace!"

Her phone buzzed. "Sorry, Rowena. I have

another call coming in. I'd better take it. I'll call you later. Bye!"

Toby trotted in from the kitchen. Clarissa was pacing the living room, her laptop already open and several photo printouts scattered over the dining table. Toby had a feeling she wouldn't be letting him watch *Murder She Wrote* on one of the Freeview channels. *Hmpf.*

"Hey, you!" she said into her phone. Her voice had changed. "You okay?"

It had to be Ed. She didn't speak like that to anyone else. Not on the phone anyway.

"Good. Are you going home now?" She listened. "Oh," she said, then "Oh," again, and this time her voice dropped a whole octave.

This doesn't sound good. Toby took his place in his new basket and stared up at Clarissa. *Has Ed been poisoned?*

"Right, but—" A pause. "And you? Oh."

Toby was itching to know what was being said. He tapped his paw, impatiently waiting for Clarissa to wrap up her conversation. "Should I come over?" Pause. "Oh. Well, no, she doesn't need a responsible adult, that's true. Alright." Another pause. "If you're sure. I'll see you when I see you. Yes. Ta-ra."

Clarissa hadn't even closed down the conversation and Toby was bolting out of his basket to her side. "What's going on?" he asked.

"You're so nosy," Clarissa complained, sinking into the sofa.

"I prefer to call it inquisitive," Toby corrected her. "What did Ed say?"

Clarissa sighed. "He said that there was an autopsy on the mayor overnight and the cause of death was consumption of a toxic substance. They've already started searching the mayor's house, and now ... the next step seems to be calling Dee Dee into the police station for a formal interview and issuing a search warrant for her premises."

"Oh dear," said Toby.

"Exactly." Clarissa pouted. "I asked if I could go with her to the police station but apparently that's not allowed. She's big enough and ugly enough to look after herself."

"I wouldn't say Dee Dee is ugly," Toby said.

"It's just an expression, Tobes."

"Okay." *Big enough and ugly enough.* Toby squirrelled that one away to use another day.

"It's horrible to think of the police going through her things."

"They won't find anything," Toby reassured her. *Not in the bakery anyway.* If there'd been anything there, he felt certain he'd have found it. Besides, the more he thought about the conversation he'd had with Sal the previous evening, the more he conceded that the rat might have a point.

"What if someone is framing Dee Dee?" Toby asked.

Clarissa's eyes burned into his. "What do you mean?"

"It's something Sal said last night."

Clarissa's forehead creased. "Nobody would be that evil, surely?"

Toby returned her stare steadily. She had to be joking! What about some of the villains they'd dealt with in the past year or so? "Somebody might have it in for her."

Clarissa shook her head. "So they have it in for her and they take it out on the mayor? Toby, that's crackers."

"The mayor's not suffering any more, is he?" Toby shrugged.

"I worry about you!"

"But if you lock Dee Dee up for a crime she didn't commit, then she'll suffer for the rest of her life."

"Huh." Clarissa raised her eyebrows and shook

her head slowly, but Toby could see activity behind her eyes. She was thinking about what he'd said.

"Do you know if she has any enemies?" Toby asked. "Me and Sal were discussing this and we know she hasn't lived here very long—"

"She's worked with builders and decorators," Clarissa said, "trying to get the shop ready. And she's had dealings with the council to get the relevant licences. And ... I think she joined a yoga class because she asked me if I wanted to, but all that bending and breathing is not for me. Besides, I get enough exercise accompanying you on your walks."

Toby pricked his ears up. She'd mentioned the 'W' word. There could be no coming back from that. He began to wag his tail, slowly at first and then faster and faster.

However, Clarissa didn't appear to notice. She was chewing the inside of her cheek and staring into the distance. "I can't think of anyone else. Except ..."

Toby stopped his tail from exerting itself unnecessarily. "Except?" he asked.

"Dee Dee is very accepting of the other bakers." Clarissa jumped up and hurried to the dining table to snatch up her notepad. "She told me that during our interview, remember? I wrote it down. How many bakeries did she say there were?" Flicking through some pages impatiently, she tutted. "I can't see it. Was it five or six?"

Toby nodded, feeling wonderfully wise. This was exactly what he'd been thinking.

"She may be accepting of having six or so competitors, but that doesn't mean her competitors accept *her*, does it?"

"Exactly!" said Toby, practically exploding with pride that he'd cracked the case first.

"Do you know what we should do?" Clarissa perked up.

"What?"

"Go and chat to the other bakers ..."

Toby started his tail up again. "That sounds like a great idea." Not least because he might get freebies at every single one of them, which would be totally pawesome.

"Can I come?" a small voice piped up.

Clarissa and Toby turned to gaze at the kitchen door. Sal stood there, scratching his belly and yawning. "Have I missed breakfast?"

"Sal says he's hungry," Toby informed Clarissa.

"Do you two ever stop eating?" Clarissa looked from Sal to Toby and back again. "We'll get something while we're out."

CHAPTER ELEVEN

"That's it." Clarissa pointed at a building on the other side of the marketplace. It had a faded canopy of pink and yellow stripes that sagged over the window.

"Cathy's Cakes," Toby read for Sal's benefit.

"It looks a bit ... sad." Clarissa reached for her phone and took a couple of snaps. She'd left her posh camera at home today because she had wanted to be semi-incognito if that was possible.

"There's plenty of people going in and out though," Toby observed. They weren't queuing around the block or anything, but footfall was steady.

The air was heady with a variety of scintillating aromas. The burger van was in situ, in pride of place in the market square and doing a roaring trade despite the fact that it wouldn't be lunchtime for another hour. There was also a kiosk selling sausages in rolls—not hot dogs per se, because these ones actually had proper meat in them rather than lips, tongues and butts—and bacon baguettes. Yum!

Toby took a good sniff. The fragrances danced around his nose and he could have created a road map for the source of every one of those flavours. Disappointingly, Cathy's Cakes did not smell as wonderful as either the burger van or the sausage man.

"Cheap," he said, wrinkling his nose.

"What is?" Clarissa asked.

"Whatever Cathy puts in her breakfasts."

Clarissa pulled a face. "Does Cathy do breakfast? I thought she was a baker."

"I can smell breakfast coming from her shop."

"Let's go and find out," Sal suggested. He didn't care about cheap goods or pricy ones, he just liked to eat.

They wandered across the market among the other shoppers and pedestrians. There weren't many stalls today because the market tended to open Wednesday to Saturday, but there were always a few stallholders trying their luck, and in decent weather this could pay off.

They reached the shop and gazed in through the window. Toby jumped up and rested his front paws on the window ledge so he could see inside.

The counter ran almost the full length of the minuscule shop. You walked in through the door and the counter was on your left. Behind it were the obligatory shelves laden with bread and cakes, mostly doughnuts and Devon Splits. At the not-so-far end of the shop was another counter with a glass front displaying bacon, sausages, eggs, beans, mush-rooms, tomatoes, black pudding and hash browns. The display above offered well-loved selections such as a 'takeaway Full English' for six pounds and ninety-nine pence, an 'any three item' breakfast for one pound ninety-nine, and a three ninety-nine gourmet roll of four breakfast items in a big Devon floured bap.

Sauce in a sachet would cost an additional fifty pence.

"I could buy a bottle of sauce for that," Clarissa muttered. "But I think three items for less than two pound is a bit of a bargain."

"I really wouldn't," said Toby.

Clarissa, undecided, hovered around the door.

"'Scuse, love." A bulky chap wearing a fluores-cent jacket squeezed past her. He represented

Cathy's Cakes' clientele, Toby decided. Builders and other labourers looking for a quick fuel stop found their way here as they passed through town or worked on the nearby construction site for the new shopping centre.

Toby poked his head around the door and observed Mr Fluorescent as he headed to the breakfast counter. "Full English, please, love," he said to the woman waiting there.

"Tea or coffee with that?" the woman asked. She had light-blue-coloured hair swirled on top of her head in a messy bun and wore a pink pinafore apron with the name Cathy embroidered across the chest.

Toby gaped in surprise. The old-fashioned-looking woman in Clarissa's photos. The one who'd attended The Magick Muffin's launch party. He glanced up at Clarissa and she nodded at him. She'd clocked it too.

"Yea please, love. Three sugars," Mr Fluorescent was saying.

"Cor," said Sal from Clarissa's pocket. "I'd have more sugar than that."

"That's already a lot of sugar," said Toby, who didn't like things too sweet.

"It certainly is," said Clarissa, who didn't like sugar in the slightest.

"The full works on your breakfast?" the woman asked, sliding a cardboard cup under the hot water machine and throwing a teabag inside, while simultaneously chucking a couple of slices of bread on a grill.

"No tomato, double beans, please."

"Right you are." The woman slid a takeaway tray into her left hand and began by adding four hash-browns, two sausages, two strips of bacon, a spoon of mushrooms, a side of black pudding, a fried egg and a double spoon of beans on the top.

Toby began to salivate. "I'm starving."

"You are not starving." Clarissa's own stomach had started to rumble.

The woman buttered the toast, added a splash of milk to the tea and squeezed a lid on it, handed over a couple of sugars and a stirrer and a wooden knife and fork, threw the toast inside a brown paper bag and tightened the lid on the takeaway breakfast. "Any sauce?"

"Nah, you're good," Mr Fluorescent said.

"Six ninety-nine, please."

The man handed over a crumpled tenner and waited for his change before hefting his breakfast in one hand and his tea in the other and hurrying out of the shop.

The woman caught Clarissa's eye. "Don't be shy," she said. But noticing Toby, she added, "No dogs though."

"Bloomin' cheek," Toby grumbled. "What does she think I'm going to do? Shoplift a piece of bread and butter pudding?"

"I would, given 'arf a chance," said Sal.

Clarissa sidestepped out of the woman's eyeline and poked Sal to make him hunker down in her pocket. "Stay out of sight," she hissed, "and you—" directed at Toby, "stand here by the door and do not move an inch. Not. One. Inch."

"Not one inch," Toby repeated. "Got it."

"Good."

Clarissa straightened her shoulders and stepped inside the shop. "Good morning," she said, as breezily as she could manage. "I'm Clarissa Page and I'm a journalist working for *The Celestine Times* in London. I wonder if I could take up a few minutes of your morning, please?"

"A journalist?" The woman didn't look impressed.

"That's right."

"With *The Times*, you say?"

Clarissa didn't repeat the Celestine bit. It could sometimes create more problems than it solved to admit that *The Celestine Times* was a newspaper for the paranormal. "That's right," she said. "I'm writing a story about—" She had to think quickly ... "about local businesses and how they manage competition. So, erm ..." *Gosh, how to spin this?* "Like ... is competition in the high street a good thing ... or not?"

"Oh," came the response. Clarissa wasn't really sure the woman understood her angle.

Maybe it was time to be more direct. "It's Cathy, isn't it?" Clarissa asked and extended her hand.

The woman took it, shaking it uncertainly. "Yes, Cathy."

"Pleased to meet you," Clarissa said. "So let me give you an example of what I'm investigating for my article." She pretended to think. "Here in Sun Valley, we have a new bakery opening up on Mayflower Lane, don't we?"

"We do." Cathy rolled her eyes.

Ah! Clarissa spotted that straight away. "And you don't think that's a good idea?"

"Look, I don't mind," said Cathy. "People should be free to start whatever business they choose, right?"

"Of course—"

"I'm not God. Other people's business is not my business. But—"

Clarissa, secretly thrilled because which journalist wouldn't be, could sense a big but coming. She pulled out her notepad and pen and interrupted Cathy. "Would you mind if I took some notes?"

"Whatever you like," Cathy said, warming to her rant. "Where was I?"

"Other people's business is not your—"

"That's right! Not my business. Cos ... like, this bakery, this has been in my family for over a hundred years. My great-great-grandfather started it. Back then it just sold bread because he was a master baker, and then he taught his son and granddaughter. Sadly, my great-grandfather was killed in the First World War so my grandma carried it on. She was the one who introduced cakes and things. My mum took over from my grandma, and now I've been in charge since my mum passed away a few years ago. It was us who introduced the breakfast counter ..."

Cathy was a talker. Clarissa couldn't complain about that.

"Has that worked for you?" Clarissa asked. "It seems popular."

"Yeah. We needed to do something to get people in here, you know? Footfall has been going down for the past twenty years really. When I was younger we'd be rammed. It would be me, Mum and Dad all fighting for space in here."

"I can imagine."

"But over the years trade has slowed down. People buy cheap bread in the supermarkets. All that pre-packaged stuff. It's not bread. More like cake." Cathy shuddered.

"That's true," Clarissa said, but all the while thinking of the many times she'd been unable to afford anything else apart from cheap bread.

"We had to cut our cloth a different way. Find a new way to attract customers, you know?"

"And you went with the breakfast counter." Clarissa nodded approvingly.

"Yeah, I buy all the ingredients cheap enough. It's not locally produced or anything. It's the lowest common denominator. It's popular with all the workers around here—there's so much building going on—so it draws them in. I make a decent profit and I pay my bills."

"That's the main thing," said Clarissa.

"Exactly. Other bakeries do their own things so we all kind of rub along, although I wish there were fewer and I could go back to baking more cakes rather than the run-of-the-mill doughnuts and bread and butter pudding. They sell well, so I've kept them on. Doughnuts are inoffensive, aren't they?"

"They're mother's milk to me," Sal squeaked.

Clarissa patted her pocket, hoping Cathy hadn't heard anything untoward.

"So you're not a fan of The Magick Muffin?" Clarissa asked, pen poised.

"I haven't visited it," Cathy said, screwing her mouth up.

Clarissa kept her face straight. She had evidence that Cathy *had* been there.

"I don't even know what she's supplying. Big muffins, is it? So I've heard. It's a novelty! And when that novelty wears off, she'll be struggling for customers just like the rest of us. Especially up Mayflower Lane."

"You think? Not a good location?"

"Yeah. I mean that poodle parlour never reopened, did it? The only shop up there that makes any money is the pharmacy."

"There's certainly a lot of demand for Goober's," Clarissa agreed. "But I think there are a few shops up there doing alright."

"I'm not sure Sun Valley needs another bakery," Cathy replied flatly. "But good luck to her." It didn't sound like she meant it though. "Anyway, I've heard she's had a bit of trouble already."

"That's true." Clarissa rearranged her face from supportive and interested to more neutral and sympathetic, unsure which emotion would work best with Cathy at this stage. "Something about someone becoming ill?"

Cathy raised her eyebrows. "Surprised you haven't heard more than that. Rumours are she hasn't opened this morning because the mayor died after eating there."

"Gosh!" Clarissa pretended to look shocked. "No way! You wouldn't have thought anyone could react so badly to a massive muffin, would you?"

Cathy laughed at that. "Unless they were a coeliac, I suppose."

"Coeliac?" The thought had never occurred to Clarissa. "That's an allergy to wheat, isn't it?"

"It's an allergy to gluten. It's important that all bakers know about these sorts of allergies cos we get customers in who want gluten-free stuff. Idiots. Who comes into a bakery of all things and expects not to find wheat? Wheat is a gluten, of course, but there are others such as barley and rye. I don't think I sell anything for coeliacs except for the tomatoes and bacon. Even my sausages have wheat in them."

"If you were coeliac, would eating a muffin kill you?" Clarissa asked.

"I don't think so." Cathy pushed her bottom lip

out and wrinkled her nose. "But I'm sure it could make some people properly poorly."

"Hmm." Clarissa made a note to find out more. "You have to sympathise with the owner of The Magick Muffin if that is the case."

"Yeah, but who needs out-of-towners coming into Sun Valley and buying our homes and running businesses? It should be down to us, the locals. And local people should support local businesses. Make sure you put that in your article." Cathy tapped the counter with an imperious finger.

"I will." Clarissa pretended to make a note but she simply scribbled nonsense. "I feel sorry for the mayor. One minute he was hale and hearty, and—"

"Oh, don't bother feeling sorry for old Casterford." Cathy wafted the air in dismissal. "Honestly, that's a waste of good grief. The man was a crook, plain and simple."

"You think?" Clarissa couldn't hide her surprise.

"I *do* think. In fact, everyone thinks the same. He'd do anything for a backhander, that man. He only got the position of mayor because he brown-nosed the local MP, council bigwigs and dignitaries. Money talks."

"I didn't know that." Now Clarissa *was* scribbling ferociously, making a note to check out the mayor's background.

"You'll find there's loads of us local businesses who never liked that man. Us *old* established businesses. Believe me, if that new woman did find a way to kill the mayor, she did us all a favour!"

CHAPTER TWELVE

"Phew." Clarissa sat on a bench with Toby by her side trying to nuzzle his way into the paper bag she was clutching. "There's a lot to unpick there. I feel like I've gone ten rounds with Tyson Fury."

"Who's he?" Toby asked, managing to inhale some of the scented air from inside the bag. *Oooooooh, that smells good!*

"Never mind." Clarissa brushed him away. "Get off. This is mine."

"What is it?" Toby watched as Clarissa drew a bun out of the bag. It was round and super squidgily soft, cut across the top to reveal a slightly yellow dough. The cut had then been stuffed full of clotted cream and a good helping of freshly made jam.

"It's a Devon Split," Clarissa told him. "My new friend Cathy was telling me this used to be her grandma's signature bake and that people would come from far and wide to enjoy the family's secret recipe." Clarissa took a huge bite. The dough was as soft as it looked and her face disappeared for a moment, the cream sliding everywhere. "Umm. Mmm." When she reappeared, she had cream on her nose and jam on her chin.

Toby stared at her in horror. "What a mess! Let me clean you up!" He stuck his tongue out and advanced.

"Get off," Clarissa said, mouth full.

Sal, now allowed out of Clarissa's pocket, chuckled. He reached out to scoop up a handful of jam and cream. "I guess we all look like rats if the treat is big enough."

Clarissa finished off most of the bun, but she did —reluctantly—save a decent-sized chunk for Toby and a smaller—much to his dismay—piece for Sal.

"My bit didn't have any jam," Toby complained.

"It barely touched the sides," Clarissa noted, cleaning her sticky hands on a tissue. "I doubt you had time to notice."

"I beg to differ," Toby replied airily. "This spell-bound hound notices *everything*."

"Is that a fact?"

"It is. For example, I noticed that Cathy didn't like newcomers or new bakers and ... drum roll please—"

Sal pretended to play the drums and made the appropriate sounds.

"She didn't like the mayor either!"

"Ba-doom-tsss!" sang Sal. "I'm not sure that woman likes anyone."

"I don't know that she'd kill the mayor," Clarissa said. "In fact, she pretty much implicated everyone else in Sun Valley."

"That'll please Ed," Toby remarked, "if he has to interview the whole town!"

"Poor Ed. We'll never see him again," Clarissa replied mournfully. "Bad enough as it is."

"Oh, she's got it bad," said Sal.

"Ick," said Toby and nudged Clarissa. "I'm your number one," he reminded her.

She laughed. "Of course you are."

Sal sniffed. "I'll never be anyone's number one." He waited for somebody—anybody—to say something encouraging, but no-one did.

"So what now?" Toby stretched, yawned and shook himself.

"I suppose we should try the next bakery on our list." Clarissa consulted her notebook.

"Good idea," said Toby. "I'm still waiting for second breakfast."

"You just had a piece of my Devon Split, you greedy young scamp."

Toby closed his eyes in exasperation. Had he taught Clarissa nothing? "That wasn't second breakfast, that was a morning treat! A second breakfast would have to include something substantial." He gazed at Clarissa with soft eyes. "Like a sossidge."

"You're never happy," Clarissa told him.

"A sossidge sammich would be even more perfect."

"Really?"

"That's my favourite favourite," Toby told her.

"This morning at least," she said, standing up and throwing her rubbish in a nearby litter bin. "We'll see. Come on."

Toby jumped off the bench and Clarissa grabbed her lead. "Where to?" he asked.

"High Street," said Clarissa. "Groggs."

"Hokay." Toby trotted ahead of Clarissa, winding in his usual leisurely fashion through the market, sniffing for peemails here and there. Not that he expected to find any. He didn't habituate the market as much as, say, the park or Chamberlain Drive and surrounds. But he was hoping to hear from Troot and his best friend, Pippin. He hadn't seen them for ages. He hoped they were okay.

The high street was a strange place, Toby often thought. It had been pedestrianised some time ago, but Old Joe claimed that pedestrianisation seemed to have sucked the life out of it. Shops were arranged on either side of the wide avenue. There were bigger stores here than along Mayflower Lane and around the market. There were banks and building societies, a high street chemist and lots of chain stores. Or rather, there were units that *had been* those things. Along with the large department store that had ceased trading a few months previously, many of them were now closed and a number of the buildings had been boarded up, meaning the entire street appeared run down despite the businesses that valiantly remained open.

Groggs was one of those.

Skateboards clattered as the trio walked down a slight incline in the direction of the bakery. Toby started from the sound and ducked away.

"It's alright," Clarissa soothed him, but as she pulled on the lead to encourage him back to his place beside her, one skater lost control of his board entirely. Throwing himself off it, the young lad rolled and jumped to his feet quickly enough, but the board shot away and smacked into Toby's backside.

Toby yelped.

"Oi!" Clarissa bellowed, shocking Toby, Sal *and* fellow pedestrians. Had she ever sounded so angry? The skater ignored her. "You just hurt my dog!" she yelled as the lad rescued the board. This time he graced Clarissa with a middle-fingered salute.

Instead of moving on, Clarissa waited and watched. As the skater mounted his board and set off again, she directed her own brand of salute in his direction. Wiggling her index finger, she accompanied it with a single burst of hot energy that knocked the lad flying and sent him sprawling face down into a pile of black rubbish bags awaiting collection outside a kebab shop. The skateboard flew up in the air. What goes up must inevitably come back down. The skateboard landed on the kid's backside with a loud whack.

The rider howled while his friends fell about laughing.

Clarissa averted her eyes and hid a smirk. "Idiot," she muttered.

"I'm alright," Toby said. "Don't worry about me."

He limped, exaggerating as much as possible. "I'll live."

"Just walk it off, mate." Sal smacked his fist into his palm. "You can do it."

"Think of the sossidge," Clarissa said and strolled on.

"Hmpf."

Groggs turned out to be a different bakery altogether in comparison to the ones that Toby was familiar with. This one was branded for starters—part of a *franchise*, Clarissa explained—and had folding glass doors that were open all the way so that the counter was almost the entire length of the shop and mere feet away from the pavement! This was a novelty to Toby. Not so much a shop as a drive-through for dogs.

It also meant he didn't have to be left outside, because outside was all there was!

Plenty of people were queuing up to be served—it was edging towards lunchtime now—but there were four assistants serving. Business was therefore slick, and Clarissa didn't have to wait long for her turn.

"Hi!" she said, smiling brightly.

"Help you?" an older chap with a tired ponytail asked.

"Is it possible to speak to the owner?" she asked.

The ponytail guy curled his lip. "There's no owner."

"A manager then?"

"You want to speak to a manager?"

"Yes." Clarissa fixed her smile. "Is that possible?"

"Sure." The ponytail guy gave her the once-over before slinking away. "Jake? Lady here wants a word."

Clarissa looked down the line of servers wondering who Jake would be. He turned out to be the youngest of the servers, an unfortunate bony specimen of teenage humanity with a spattering of acne and incredibly pale eyes and eyelashes.

"Can I help you, madam?" the kid asked.

Clarissa blinked. "You're the manager?"

He puffed himself up. "I am, yes. How may I assist?"

Toby glanced up at Clarissa as she took stock of the situation. *Game face!* he telegraphed.

"I'm Clarissa Page," she said, starting her spiel from scratch. "I'm a journalist for *The Celestine Times*—"

Something like fear crossed the kid's face. "A journalist?"

"Yes. I'm writing an article about competition among local businesses—"

"Yeah?" The young man still seemed worried. "Are you trying to blame us for taking business away from others?"

"No." Clarissa frowned. "Not at all. I'm just—"

"Because I think you probably need to speak to our head office."

"I thought you were the manager?"

"I am—"

"And the other chap said there was no owner?"

"We're franchised. I don't have authority to talk on behalf of the company."

"But you could talk on behalf of this branch, couldn't you?" Clarissa pressed.

"I wouldn't want to do that without the say-so from head office."

"I see." Clarissa could see she wasn't going to get anywhere. She tried a different tack. "Have you ever had any dealings with Mayor Casterford?"

The young man shook his head. "Who? Doesn't ring a bell."

"Mayor Casterford?" Clarissa repeated. "He passed away suddenly over the weekend."

The young man shrugged. "You'd have to speak to head office."

"Where is your head office?" Clarissa asked.

"London."

"I doubt they'd know who he is then."

The young man laughed. "*I* don't know who he is and I live here. Plus, let's face it, head office don't know who I am and I work for them. Sorry. I can't help you."

This was becoming abundantly clear. "Do you have a number for head office?" Clarissa asked.

"It's on the website," the young man said. "Now, if you'll excuse me." He took three steps sideways. "Yes, madam?" he asked a woman standing behind Clarissa. "Can I help you?"

"Unlikely," muttered Clarissa. "Grrrrrr."

Toby stared up at her. *Is she growling?* "Erm—" He cleared his throat. "No chance of a sossidge—"

"Let's get out of here, Toby. I've had enough of this place!"

CHAPTER THIRTEEN

"This is my last one for today," Clarissa said. "What Cathy said about Casterford is bugging me. I want to find out more about him."

They were approaching a bakery on the same road as the florist across from the park but further down and away from Chamberlain Drive. Clarissa always called this the posh part of town for some reason. Toby couldn't understand why. The mini-mart they used was on this road, and there was an old newsagent and tobacconist shop that Toby always thought smelled appealing. These businesses weren't upmarket in the slightest. She had explained it was posh—from her point of view—because there was a handful of high-end shops here, including a bridal boutique, a stereo shop and a specialist beauty salon.

Clarissa had never set foot in any of them. They scared her.

"Plus my feet are hurting and I'm thirsty," she grumbled. The kid in Groggs had really annoyed her.

"At least you've eaten," Toby replied, also a tad snarkily. "Some of us are wasting away."

"Absolutely." Sal patted his stomach. It jiggled like a jelly.

"And you didn't get run over by a skateboard," Toby pointed out. "I might have been wiped out. Permanently!"

"But you weren't and you'll be absolutely fine," Clarissa promised him. "I'll buy you a snack soon, okay?"

"I'm holding you to that," Toby said, and trotted along a little more perkily.

"Bryn's Bakes." Clarissa pointed it out. "Oooh. That looks fancy, doesn't it?" They stopped a little distance away to admire it.

This bakery had a frontage that exceeded even the width of Groggs and a sun canopy that put Cathy's Cakes to shame. In orange and dark brown stripes, it screamed classy. Beneath the canopy was a small terrace of sturdy but aesthetically appealing tables and benches surrounded by troughs of flowers. The window glass was tinted in a brown colour but the lights were on inside the shop, and even from their vantage, they could see shining surfaces and bottles, while the window was laden with beautiful cake displays.

"This does look nice," Clarissa said, and when she started to walk again, her step was jaunty. Music, soft and jazzy, Spanish or Cuban perhaps, spilled out from the shop. Couples and pairs of women sat at the tables sipping coffee and eating cakes and sandwiches.

Toby did the sniff test and found roast ham, roasted vegetables, grilled halloumi—which he'd once tried and been incredibly disappointed by—houmous, other cheeses—although could you genuinely call something as rubbery as halloumi a cheese?—salads and an array of different cakes and breads scenting the air. He began salivating. Even the bread smelt less like bread and more like ...

"Mmmm. Focaccia. Wow. Look at all these Italian breads!" Clarissa groaned.

Toby peered inside the window. *Very artisan*, he thought, and had a go at reading the little display cards with the names of the breads carefully handwritten on them. *Crescentina. That's easy enough. Bread shaped like the moon. Pane Pugliese. Something to do with a window and a pug? What an odd name. Pane di Segale. A pain of seagulls? Is that what a group of them is known as? Oh. Well, lots of people think seagulls are a pain in the—*

"I do love focaccia," Clarissa said, sighing. "Proper bread, this!"

"It's a good job Dee Dee can't hear you say that," Toby said.

"I like British bread too!" Clarissa pointed to the shelves. "See, they have all sorts there. Cottage. Split tin. Milk loaf. They don't sound as romantic as the Italian names though."

"Yes, but you eat bread, you don't marry it," Toby couldn't help pointing out. "It doesn't have to be romantic."

"I'd marry a cheese and onion loaf any day of the week," said Sal.

"Come to that, so would I," Toby agreed. "Especially if it had been sliced up to make cheese sammiches. You can't beat a cheese sammich. They really are my favourite favourites."

"You can bring your dog inside!" A cheerful woman with an orange and dark-brown apron beamed at Clarissa. "As long as they don't make their way around the back of the counter, you'll be fine."

"Thank you," said Clarissa, and Toby scampered inside with her. "Best behaviour!" Clarissa told him.

"Boy or a girl?" the woman asked and slipped behind the counter, where she opened a glass jar and plucked out several treats.

"A boy," Clarissa told her. "Toby."

"So cute."

Toby preened.

The woman handed over the treats. Toby smiled up at Clarissa expectantly, but Clarissa held on to them.

Had she forgotten he existed? "Erm ... hello?"

"Looks like a schnauzer," the serving lady said.

"Thanks! Yes, he's a ... schnauzery whippety thingie."

"Whatever he is, he's lovely!" The woman laughed. "Can I help you with anything?"

"My name's Clarissa Page and I'm a journalist with *The Celestine Times*. I don't suppose the owner's about, are they?"

"Bryn? I can give him a shout if you like," the woman said. "He's upstairs in the office."

"I'd appreciate that, thank you." Clarissa turned her attention to a stand of baked goods beside her: Ciriola, brioche, Babà Rustica ... jars of olive oil ... sweets in bright wrappers ...

The woman hurried away and picked up a phone. She spoke into it and a moment later was back with them. "He'll come down. He suggested you take a seat and enjoy a coffee on the house. What can I get you?"

"Just a filter coffee, please. I'm no aficionado."

"No problem. Even our filter coffee is wonderful." The woman smiled and indicated the terrace. "Make yourself comfortable. I'll be with you in a moment."

Clarissa headed outside and chose a table on the edge. "Look at this, Toby," she marvelled. "Cushions! A bit different to the other two bakeries we've visited this morning."

"Completely different," Toby agreed. *There isn't a sossidge to be seen here!* He began to clamber up beside Clarissa but she pushed him down.

"Probably better if you keep all four paws on the floor. It's a bit too nice here to allow dogs on the furniture."

Toby could hardly believe his furry ears. "Too nice? That's not *nice* at all!"

"Ssssh!" Clarissa scolded. The woman who had taken her order was heading towards them, carrying a tray. She placed a glass pot of filter coffee on the table along with a mug-shaped, hand-crafted cup, a saucer, a jug of milk, a teeny bowl of sugar cubes and a glass of water. She finished off with a plate with some square chunks of almond biscotti and another arranged with a few more dog treats.

Clarissa clapped her hands. "Oooh! Thank you so much!"

"You're welcome. Enjoy!" The woman bustled away while Clarissa examined her biscotti. So fresh! "I think I want to move in here."

"I don't," Toby grumbled from under the table, but Clarissa soothed him with a bone-shaped treat.

She'd only managed a couple of mouthfuls of coffee when a man ambled over to the table. Clarissa didn't see him coming and, startled, slopped her coffee into her saucer.

The man chuckled. "Sorry, sorry!" Dressed in raspberry-coloured trousers, a cream shirt with pink and blue threads running through it, a banana-coloured cravat, and with his thinning hair brushed away from his tanned face, he looked like someone who enjoyed sailing regattas and gin and tonics at the yacht club. But he had friendly eyes and a winning smile. "Bryn Burns. You're the journalist, are you?" He held out a hand.

Clarissa took it and shook. "Clarissa Page," she told him. "I'm with *The Celestine Times* in London."

"You're a distance from home, then."

"I'm the regional correspondent for the South West."

"Ah. I see. That makes sense. What can I do for you?"

"I'm writing an article about competition on the high street," Clarissa said, feeling oddly guilty to be lying yet again. "About whether it's a good thing or a bad thing when so many businesses have to close. I have a theory that a certain amount of competition can be healthy because people are drawn to towns that specialise. Like Hay-on-Wye, for example, with all its bookshops or ... erm ... Glastonbury with its New Age shops and ... erm ... things." The more she thought about it, the better she thought this article could be. It would be worth pitching it to Rowena.

"Sounds interesting. May I?" Bryn indicated the bench opposite Clarissa.

"Of course!" Clarissa reached for her notepad and a pen.

Bryn slid onto the bench, managing to tread on Toby's paw in the process.

"Owwwwwww! You great clumsy oaf!" Toby complained.

"Oh, my goodness!" Bryn was beside himself. "I am *so* sorry. I didn't see you had a dog under there."

"Owwwwwwww!"

"My fault," Clarissa said, fumbling for Toby. "Shhh, Toby!"

"He's broken my toes!"

"He hasn't broken your toes!" she hissed.

"Crushed to a pulp they are!"

Clarissa glanced over at Bryn and grimaced. "I do apologise. He can be a little overdramatic. I think it's the whippet part of him."

Bryn laughed, his face flushed pink. "I understand. I used to have a greyhound who sounded like he was being murdered if you even looked at him wrong."

"I'm not that bad," said Toby, holding up his paw. "But this is damaged beyond repair!"

Bryn reached for one of the treats on the saucer and held it out to Toby. "Sorry, sunshine. Can we be friends?"

Toby considered this for a moment before accepting the treat. "Alright," he said. "Peace out."

"Maybe you'd better tell him you have a rat, too," said Sal from deep within Clarissa's denim jacket pocket. "Just in case he tries to crush me."

"He'd have to get extraordinarily close to Clarissa to do that, Sal!" Toby told him. "I don't think Ed would be pleased."

"He's a vocal chap, isn't he?" Bryn remarked.

"Yes, he loves the sound of his own voice," Clarissa replied. "Now, where were we?" She glared down at Toby. "Shush."

"My lips are sealed," Toby said.

Satisfied, Clarissa took a breath and picked up her pen. Might as well jump in at the deep end. "You have a beautiful place here."

"Thank you." Bryn smiled. "I've worked hard over the past two years to get it to where I want it to be."

"Have you always been a baker?"

"Man and boy. My family have been bakers in Sun Valley for generations. I split away from the family business to do something different. I'd spent time in Italy as a young man and knew I wanted to learn how to produce their breads and cakes, so when I had the opportunity, I went back and studied there. It helps that I have an Italian wife, so she was able to help me with the nitty-gritty of work permits, official communication and so on ... Oh! And translation where needed. And boy was it needed. I speak a little Italian, but not a huge amount."

"Fascinating!" said Clarissa. "So your family baked British style or—"

"Yes, just your run-of-the-mill bread and cakes."

"Quite a change for you."

"It was. But you know, it was a dream come true to finally secure these premises and create Bryn's Bakes. I probably should have called it something Italian, but I wanted my name above the door."

"And you chose to stay in Sun Valley, despite there already being a number of bakeries here?"

"As you can see, Bryn's Bakes is not in competition with anyone. Well, having said that, I expect the new baker will give me a run for my money."

Clarissa hid her sudden excitement. "What makes you say that?"

"The owner's a talented baker. I popped over there for her launch, and I was impressed by her offering."

"You were there?" Clarissa checked.

"Not for long because we were short-staffed here. My wife, Maria, wasn't feeling well so I needed to help cover."

"I'm sorry to hear that. I hope she's feeling better now?"

"Yes, she's back to her usual bubbly self, thank you," Bryn confirmed.

Clarissa tapped her pen against her teeth. "Are you worried about the competition in town?"

"Mmmm." Bryn wobbled his head. "Not really. Perhaps a little. I think what we offer here and what you can get elsewhere is markedly different, so in that regard, there's room for all of us."

"But you said"—Clarissa checked her notes—"the new baker will give you a run for your money?"

"In terms of quality and excitement, yes. Fabulous flavours. Something different. Absolutely she will. But also, I think she's different enough that we'll each have customers who prefer us to any other baker or who think both of us are the dog's doo-dahs!"

Toby stared out from under the table. "You can leave my doo-dahs out of this, bud."

Clarissa poked him with her toe.

"It's a shame that she's had a bit of trouble over the weekend," Bryn added. "That's not what a new business needs. I hope she gets back to work soon."

"You heard about the mayor, then?" Clarissa asked, glad he'd brought it up.

"I think everyone has heard about Casterford by now," Bryn said. "It's all anyone was talking about this morning."

"Did you know him?"

Bryn curled his lip. "I didn't *know* him, but I'd certainly had some dealings with him. I had to set my lawyers on him about ten or twelve years ago now. My mother needed some permissions from the council for the bakery we had up on Lewin Street." Seeing Clarissa's blank face, he added, "Up near the big housing estate? We had one of the units up there."

"Oh, I know." Clarissa could picture it. Vaguely.

"He was insinuating she wouldn't get the relevant permits unless she gave him a backhander. A thoroughly unpleasant man."

"I see."

"I reported him to the council and they didn't do anything. Said there must have been a mistake. Yeah, right. Absolute nonsense."

Another black mark for the mayor!

"And you don't rate the other bakers in town?" Clarissa checked her list. "Groggs? Cathy's Cakes? Scrumpy Dumpy's?"

"I think of Groggs as more of a fast-food outfit than a bakery, to be honest. They heat up goods in the shop but their production happens in a massive factory." Bryn dismissed them out of hand. "Decent quality for a decent price, sure. But low-end. And that's fine. They do a job and they attract their own market."

Clarissa nodded. *And the customer service is absolutely rubbish*, she thought.

"Scrumpy Dumpy's is delightful. A wonderful

old bakery. I highly recommend it to anyone. Old Liss—have you met her yet?"

"No." Scrumpy Dumpy's would be Clarissa's first stop tomorrow.

"She's fabulous. You know, she must be in her seventies but she's still going strong. I love her, although to be honest, we haven't had much to do with each other for a few years."

"And Cathy's Cakes?"

A cloud passed over Bryn's face. He didn't immediately answer.

"You don't rate Cathy?" Clarissa guessed.

"Not really." Bryn looked glum. "I'd really rather this didn't end up in your article though."

"Of course not," Clarissa said, closing her notepad and dropping her pen onto the table. *But do spill the tea*, she thought.

"It wouldn't bother me if Cathy's Cakes disappeared off the face of the earth," Bryn said, then, on seeing the look on Clarissa's face, added, "I know that sounds harsh, but we have a lot of history. That bakery should have come to me, but Cathy created such a stink about it—"

"Cathy being ...?"

"My sister."

"Ah." *Good gracious.*

"Six years ago my family owned three bakeries around Sun Valley, and the idea was that when my mother passed away, Cathy and I would sell one and each of us take one on. This was all agreed with my mother's blessing. While I was away in Italy a few years ago, my mother passed—"

"I'm sorry to hear that," Clarissa said, but Bryn barely heard her, so caught up in his story was he.

"I came home for the funeral, of course, and left everything in Cathy's capable hands when I returned to wrap up affairs in Europe. But by the time I moved back to Sun Valley permanently, Cathy had sold two of the three bakeries and kept the marketside one for herself."

"Oh dear," Clarissa sympathised. "Could she do that without your permission?"

"Apparently so. I had a lawyer check it all out, but my mother had given Cathy power of attorney and Cathy had set the wheels in motion while my mother was still alive. There was nothing I could do."

Clarissa was horrified. "But that's just ... wrong!"

"Absolutely it is! I did manage to claw some money back, which helped me to buy the lease on this place, but still. It was hurtful."

"I get that."

"So in answer to your question about competition and whether I mind it, not at all." Bryn threw his head back and laughed. "But if Cathy went out of business, I wouldn't give a rat's backside!"

"Excuse me," said Sal, wriggling in Clarissa's pocket. She hurriedly covered her chest with one hand.

"And if I never see Cathy again, I won't care!" declared Bryn. "She's poisonous!"

CHAPTER FOURTEEN

"I reckon I'd be happy living in Italy," Sal said. He and Toby were moonbathing on top of the wizarding shed. "Imagine the scene ... Sparkling seas, blue skies, biscotti biscuit crumbs absolutely everywhere ..."

"Pizza crusts," Toby added. "Yum."

"Cheese," said Sal. "So much cheese!"

"Meatballs." Toby sighed.

"Shall we emigrate?" Sal asked.

"I doubt Clarissa would. She likes it here. She's not fond of the sun. Plus Ed's here, isn't he? At the moment she wouldn't leave him behind."

They both poked their tongues out. "Bleugh."

"I thought you liked the Ed hooman?" asked Moriarty. She was sitting primly on the highest point of the shed, probably listening out for mousing opportunities.

"We do," said Toby.

"He's a sweetheart," said Sal.

"A bit of a fool at times," said Toby.

"But we don't hold that against him," Sal added.

"It's just all that lovey-dovey stuff." Toby pulled a face again.

"Ick," said Sal.

"Perhaps you could all move out there together," suggested Moriarty. "Ed as well."

"Do they have detectives in Italy?" asked Sal.

"I think the Pink Panther came from there." Toby scratched his head. "Oh, wait. Maybe he was French."

"It's all the same to me," said Sal. "Oo-row-pee-on."

"Speaking of detectives," said Moriarty, "where are you up to with this bakery case?"

"I think we found out quite a lot today," Toby said, thinking back over the day's events. Clarissa was inside writing up her notes. "We discovered that Cathy doesn't like Dee Dee and Bryn doesn't like Cathy and the staff at Groggs don't know anything about anything and they really don't care either and nobody but nobody liked Mayor Casterford."

"A fair summation," said Sal, scratching his belly. Toby was beginning to wonder whether Sal had fleas.

"But how does that help you?" Moriarty asked.

"I'm not sure," Toby admitted. "I still don't know whether Dee Dee is guilty or innocent, and I don't know whether anyone is trying to set Dee Dee up to take a fall—"

"If they were trying to set her up, my money would be on Cathy," said Sal.

"Would it?" Toby scrunched up his face, not so sure.

"Yeah. She didn't seem like a happy lady. Unhappy people do unhappy things ..."

"I'm not sure that follows," said Moriarty, inspecting her claws. "I'm fairly sure happy people can do unhappy things too."

"Unhappy as in murderous?" Toby asked. "Let's be clear about what we're suggesting here."

"Ladies are more likely to be poisoners than men," Sal reminded Toby. He'd been watching lots of afternoon detective shows too, so he knew what he was talking about.

"I don't know." Toby shook his head. "I know she wasn't the nicest of people"—mainly because she didn't like dogs—"but I didn't get a sense that she would murder anyone."

"I think Toby has a soft spot for the ladies," said Sal.

"Not the pointy ones," Toby said.

"Why don't you go and take a look at this Cathy's premises?" Moriarty suggested.

"What, now?" Toby had been considering a pre-nighttime nap. Setting out on an adventure wasn't high on his list of priorities right now.

"No time like the present," said Moriarty.

Sal didn't appear too keen either. He began slinking towards the ladder stairs. "I just need to check on my bottle-top collection."

"What bottle-top collection?" Toby had never seen Sal with a collection of any kind. He reached out a paw and blocked Sal's progress. "I'll need you in case I can't gain entry in any legitimate way—"

"Breaking in is never going to be legitimate," huffed Sal. "Even if you use magick, it's still breaking in."

Toby ignored this and turned to Moriarty. "Why don't you come with us? We could use a lookout."

Moriarty stared back at him, her green eyes glinting. "I'm so sorry," she said. "I can't tonight. I'm washing my hair."

"When you look closely at this place, you can see it's a bit rough and ready, can't you?" Toby sniffed along the bottom of the entrance to Cathy's Cakes. Like many of the shops that faced onto the market, the bakery had iron shutters over the windows, while the door had one of those external blinds that you pull down. It didn't reach all the way to the bottom —not quite—and so the wood of the door was exposed. Rotten and damp. Toby had a theory it might disintegrate if he sneezed. "I wonder why she decided to keep this shop when she sold the other two ..."

"Maybe this is where it all started." Sal sat back on his haunches and gazed up. This was a three-storey dwelling, built a long time ago. The walls were uneven and the mortar had rotted away and fallen out in places. There was no double glazing, just old-fashioned single-pane windows in a tall Georgian style.

"You're probably right," Toby said. "Cathy was feeling sentimental."

"Not sentimental enough to cut her bruvver some slack with his inheritance though!" Sal laughed. "Sounds like me and my bruvvers."

"You have brothers?" Toby had never considered this before.

"Not many. Only a couple o' hundred."

"Let's hope they don't all want to come and stay at Christmas," said Toby. He could only imagine Clarissa's reaction to that.

"I don't suppose they'd ever bovver," said Sal and changed the subject before Toby could pry anymore. "Are we going in this way?"

"I don't think so," said Toby. "There has to be a back entrance. Let's go and find it."

Sticking to the shadows, the odd pair scurried the full length of the marketplace. Toby kept an eye out for Pippin, but she didn't materialise. He figured she must have left town because otherwise he'd have heard her on the Twilight Barking from time to time.

They cut around the back and along the alley until they found what they were looking for. A sign written by whoever had painted the one above the shop window. Same logo of Devon Splits with gaudy-coloured jam. *Cathy's Cakes. Deliveries,* the sign read.

"This is it." Toby led the way, fully prepared to use his magick to gain entry. But there was no need. The door had been left slightly ajar.

"Oh," said Toby, stopping still.

"Uh-oh," said Sal. He caught a handful of Toby's fur and balanced alongside his friend. They craned their necks. There was a light on upstairs. It shone through a narrow window on the first floor. "Someone's in."

"Obviously someone's in if the door's open," Toby whispered. "There's no light on down here though. Why leave it open?"

"Cos it's a nice neighbourhood?" Sal suggested.

"Yeah, that's right. It's a nice neighbourhood in the back alley but a rough neighbourhood out in the market and that's why the front has shutters and the back door is wide open," Toby replied, his low voice laden with sarcasm.

"Alright, keep your shirt on," Sal replied grumpily. "Not many people will come down this way. I'm just sayin'."

Toby thought about this. Sun Valley wasn't the rough streets of LA, was it? It wasn't downtown Bangkok or the back alleys of New York. It wasn't even Birmingham on a Saturday night. Sal might have a point.

"Let's have a quick peep," Toby said, keeping his voice low. "First hint of movement and we're out of there."

"I hope we don't come across any more crazy rats," Sal said.

Toby gave Sal a sideways glance. "Yeah. I've had enough of them to last me a lifetime."

Using his snout, he edged the back door open, Sal clinging on to his tail and listening out for an alarm. If there was an alarm it hadn't been set, so they proceeded into the rear of the shop. Now that they'd been inside Dee Dee's bakery, they weren't surprised by what they found. Right here, at the door, was a kind of boot room where coats and shoes were stored along with a bucket and mop that smelt of disinfectant, a dustpan and brush, and a shelf piled high with what looked like—from their vantage point—tea towels or something similar.

Moving on, they found themselves in the bakery. The ovens, much older than the ones in The Magick Muffin but still easily identifiable, occupied most of one wall. The preparation table took up a sizable portion of the wall shopside. On the wall nearest the back door was the fridge and lots of wooden shelving, with sacks and barrels piled up alongside. The centre of the room was dominated by wooden slatted shelves on wheels. The whole place was cosy due to the restricted amount of space.

"Let's have a look around," Toby whispered, so

they separated and began sniffing the rough stone floor, each heading in a different direction. Toby made a beeline for the fridge. It had been cleaned—the whole place had—and yet there was a residual smell of raw bacon coming from here. It wasn't unpleasant, although in his opinion, bacon is far better when cooked. The same could be said for sausages. He could also smell cream. Clotted cream. And jam. Strawberry.

On a shelf way above his head he could smell eggs. These hadn't been washed, and the whiff of hen clung to them for those with a discerning nose. The barrels contained flour and sugar. Nothing else.

The scents in Cathy's Cakes were simpler to discern than the ones in Dee Dee's bakery, that was for sure. There didn't appear to be anything out of the ordinary. No poison wrappers. No cyanide in a jar labelled *Toxic!*

Hmmm. "I'm going to have a look in the front," Toby whispered and approached the connecting door. Once again, it was already open.

Toby frowned. Presumably Cathy didn't keep much cash on the premises, but even so ... why hadn't she secured the shop?

He crept out into the small space between the front and back of the shop, like Dee Dee's divided by doors with the stairs going up between them. He could see the yellow of the light falling on the walls halfway up the stairs, but down here everything was just shadow and he had to rely mainly on smell.

Ahead of him the bakery was still and quiet, the only light coming from the streetlights bleeding through the iron shutters over the window. Even with this limited illumination, Toby could see that the counters—particularly the breakfast counter right in front of him—were gleaming. Cathy took pride in keeping her premises ship-shape.

He inhaled. Pine disinfectant. Faint traces of strawberry and vanilla. Cooked meat. And ... something else ...

Toby backed out of the shop and turned his attention to the stairs. He could hear voices. Faint. None of them belonged to Cathy. It had to be the television or the radio. No movement. Cathy would be lounging on her sofa—just as he and Clarissa and now Sal liked to do—watching one of those soaps where everyone argued all the time. Except when they first met and were lovely to each other, but then they'd get married and argue all the time and then at Christmas they'd be bickering non-stop, and then one of them would die ...

Toby pricked his ears, listening for even the

slightest rustle of clothing or a hiss of breath. Anything.

But there was nothing.

Maybe ... just maybe, Cathy had found the show so boring she'd fallen asleep. He put a paw on the first stair.

"What are you doing?" Sal hissed.

"I'm going to take a look upstairs."

"Are you crazy? What if you get caught? You know she doesn't like dogs!"

"What's she going to do? Put me in a pie?" Toby scoffed, although had he known about the Demon Barber of Fleet Street, perhaps he wouldn't have been so scathing.

"Ya never know!" Sal wrung his paws together.

"You stay here. Keep an eye out." Toby didn't think he needed a security guard, but it was a good way to keep Sal quiet. Despite the rat's continuing protests, he began climbing the stairs. Slowly. Quietly. Ears pricked.

"Garry! What ya doin'? I've told ya! Garry!" a woman on the television squawked. "Get back 'ere! Garry!"

If I was Garry, I wouldn't come back in a hurry either, thought Toby, halfway up the stairs by now. *I'd be running in the opposite direction.* He moved out of the shadow and into the light. Another few steps and he was officially upstairs. The atmosphere seemed to shift, become thicker somehow and, despite the music blaring away in the background as the credits began to roll on Cathy's television programme, everything seemed incredibly still and oddly quiet.

Toby stepped onto the landing straight into an open-plan lounge-kitchen-diner. Although the curtains had yet to be drawn, the lounge to his left was lit by a pair of lamps. Elsewhere on this floor, it was dark. There was no sign of Cathy on the sofa. The television played to itself.

Toby looked right towards the kitchen. A counter blocked his eyeline, but he knew ...

There was a puddle on the floor, a mug lying on its side, the handle broken off. *Bakers do it cos they knead the dough*, the mug said.

Toby stared at the mug and at the puddle.

"I smell death," he whispered. "I smell death!"

CHAPTER FIFTEEN

"What are you doing out here?" Ed asked as he exited the bakery and snapped off a pair of latex gloves. "It's getting on for three in the morning!"

"I couldn't sleep." Clarissa shivered, Toby's lead wrapped around her wrist. The early morning air had a definite chill to it.

"You should go home and go to bed," Ed told her, reaching out to rub her shoulder. "It would be nice if one of us could get some sleep!"

"I second that," said Toby.

"And I third it," said Sal from within Clarissa's denim jacket pocket.

"But I told you, I only spoke to her this morning. No, that was yesterday morning now, wasn't it? Or was it? Oh, wherever we are now—" Clarissa tapped her head in confusion. "It's been the longest day."

"You did tell me you'd spoken to her, and I understand," Ed said. "But Cathy's death is not your fault."

"How did she die?" Clarissa asked.

"You know I can't say anything about an ongoing case." Ed arched an eyebrow. "You being a journalist *and* my girlfriend."

"Oh." Clarissa pouted. "I just feel so bad. Like I brought it on her. I mean ... is it connected to the mayor's death?"

Ed surreptitiously looked around and dropped into a crouch, ostensibly to fuss Toby. Clarissa joined him down there. "There's a handsome boy," said Ed, scruggling Toby's ears. To Clarissa, in a low voice, he added, "I think so. It's looking a lot like poison."

"Might she have poisoned herself?" whispered Clarissa, who'd been considering Cathy her prime suspect.

"Anything is possible. At the moment we have no idea. It looks like she'd finished cleaning the shop and mopped the floor. Then she'd gone upstairs to make herself a drink. She must have been expecting to go back downstairs and lock up, maybe get prepared for today's baking, but she didn't make it."

"How awful."

"The scene of crime officers are waiting to go up there. I expect we'll be moving the body in a moment."

"Poor Cathy." A tear trickled down Clarissa's cheek.

"Go home," Ed told her. "Honestly. You can't do anything here, and I'm worried about you. I'll come and take a statement in the morning." He smiled. "It'll be a good excuse to see you."

"I'm beginning to feel like the common denominator here," Clarissa said, ignoring Ed's entreaty. "First I interview Dee Dee and the mayor is poisoned and then Dee Dee is under suspicion and her bakery can't open and ... and ..."

"And breathe," Toby reminded her.

"And then I interview Cathy and now she's dead."

"But you didn't kill her," Ed said. Cocking his head, he asked, "Did you?"

"This is no joking matter, Ed," Clarissa replied, sounding annoyed. But she had stopped crying, so that was something.

"Yeah, Ed! Be serious!" Toby told him. "If everyone we interviewed yesterday ends up dead then you're gonna need a bigger morgue!"

"Eek!" Clarissa clamped her hands across her mouth, eyes wide.

"What?" Ed jumped up in alarm. "What's the matter?"

"Everyone we interviewed yesterday! What if more of them end up dead?"

"That's what I'm trying to say," Toby said.

Ed shook his head. "You're getting this all out of proportion, Clarissa. This has nothing to do with you—"

"As a fellow detective, I'm here to tell you that you have to consider all eventualities, Ed," Toby told him. "For all you know, Clarissa could be the cause."

"Shut up, Toby," said Clarissa, standing up to face Ed. "I spoke to Bryn Burns at Bryn's Bakes yesterday too."

"Posh," noted Ed.

"He's Cathy's brother."

Ed took a moment to consider that information. "Okay. That's good to know."

"Maybe you should pop around there and check he's still breathing, Ed," Toby suggested.

"That's a good idea, Tobes," Clarissa agreed. "Ed? You need to make sure Bryn's alright."

"Welfare check," said Toby. He knew about

those from watching police YouTube videos on Clarissa's laptop when she wasn't around.

"Welfare check," Clarissa repeated.

"Mmm. Well ... okay ... if he's the next of kin, I can make certain someone goes around there anyway." He scanned the police cars lining the marketplace. "Who else did you talk to yesterday?"

"Oh dear," Clarissa wailed.

"Not that I'm suggesting anyone else is going to come to harm," Ed inserted hurriedly.

"The kid in Groggs."

"Kid?"

"Some rude, spotty, unhelpful nerd who just happened to be the manager," Clarissa grumped. She had yet to forgive him.

"Sounds like you wouldn't mind if he *had* coughed it." The corners of Ed's mouth twitched.

"Ed!" Clarissa sounded outraged, but Toby had to giggle.

"She didn't like him. Not one bit," he said.

"I like everyone," Clarissa protested. Which was a whopping great fib.

"Any idea what his name was?" Ed asked.

"Harry Terribly Unhelpful," Clarissa sniped. "No, I mean, he had a name badge on but I can't remember."

"Okay, well I'll get that checked out as well. Now will you go home?"

"If you insist—"

"I do." Ed pointed in the direction of Chamberlain Drive. "I'd take you myself, but—"

"Don't be silly," Clarissa told him. "We'll be fine." She considered leaning in for a kiss but decided against it. Not while Ed was on duty. "Come on, Toby."

Toby wagged his tail for Ed and turned to walk back across the market. He led Clarissa up Mayflower Lane. The Magick Muffin was still and quiet, as was Sweet Pea's Parlour for Pampered Pooches. In fact, the entire street was eery at this time of night. Toby found himself thinking about Pippin and Troot, Pickle the poodle, Peony, and now Dee Dee.

Friends may come and friends may go but death is a constant, thought Toby.

He decided not to tell Clarissa this. He couldn't imagine it would cheer her up much.

CHAPTER SIXTEEN

"They've taken Dee Dee in for questioning," Ed told Clarissa the next morning.

It was twenty to eleven and Ed had woken Clarissa not ten minutes ago. His shift had run over due to the previous night's events, and his hooded eyes and grey skin demonstrated how shattered he must be feeling. Clarissa didn't look a whole lot better. Dressed in her sleep shirt and a pair of shorts, her eyes were puffy and red-rimmed. Sitting cross-legged on the sofa, she stared at Ed—replete in a crumpled suit, a stained shirt and his tie at half mast—in horror.

"What for?"

"There's CCTV footage from around the

marketplace that shows Dee Dee was out and about yesterday evening."

"Doing what?"

"Mooching."

"Mooching?" Clarissa's voice began to rise. "Is mooching a crime now?"

Ed reached out and squeezed her knee. Toby watched carefully. There's squeezing a person's knee and there's crushing a person's knee, and Toby wanted to ensure Clarissa would still be able to walk him later. "Of course not. It's just it looks a little suspicious, given what happened to Cathy."

"And what did happen to Cathy?" Clarissa asked. "Do you know for sure yet?"

"Autopsy this morning," Ed said, rubbing his eyes. "They should be finished by lunchtime."

"But you think it's poison?"

"That's what they're saying. I assume they can guess just by looking at the body."

"Guessing is for amateurs," Toby said.

"I'm sure they'll be running tests," Clarissa told him.

"Of course they will," said Ed. "Guessing is for amateurs."

Toby nodded in a self-satisfied way. "What did I tell you? I'm not WPDCD Silverwind for nothing."

"What?" Clarissa looked confused.

"Guessing—" Ed began to repeat.

"No, not you. The furry fruit loop."

"Ah." Ed yawned. "Of course." He chuckled and reached out to stroke Toby's head. "Poor lad. The names she calls you!" He stretched. "I'd better be getting home. I'm done in, but I need to be back at work this evening so I should at least try and get some shut-eye in the meantime."

"You can sleep here if you like," Clarissa told him.

Ed raised an eyebrow and smiled. "I *really* need to sleep."

Clarissa tsked. "We won't disturb you. I have to go out, but when I get back I can cook you something."

"Mmm." Ed gave it some lengthy consideration. Toby couldn't work out whether Ed was pleased about the invitation or not. "That would save me travelling time, wouldn't it? Sounds good. I don't suppose ... Do you have any cereal? I could do with lining my stomach before I turn in, and as much as I'd like a snifter, I think it had better be something innocuous."

In-ock-you-us. Toby spelt that out in his head. It didn't look right. He'd have to consult his dictionary.

"Sure." Clarissa pushed herself reluctantly off the sofa and padded barefoot into the kitchen.

Ed's phone began to ring. "Urgh." He reached for it and stared at the screen. "Oh lord." Tapping the screen, he answered. "Plum." He listened, then replied, "Hi, Sam. Yep. Yep. Just got off. Aha. Uh. Right."

Toby watched Ed rub his forehead and then close his eyes.

Weary, thought Toby. *He looks weary. Maybe I'll treat him to some Toby snuggles when he gets into bed. Everybody sleeps better with Toby snuggles.*

"Uh-huh," Ed said. "Crikey." He glanced towards the kitchen where Clarissa could be heard clattering bowls and opening the fridge. "Do you have a description?"

A longer pause, until Ed blew out his cheeks. "Rightio. I'll get over there."

Clarissa returned to the living room clutching two bowls of cornflakes. Toby pouted. *Shouldn't that be three?*

"What was that?" Clarissa asked. "Did you just say you were leaving?"

Toby pricked his ears up. If Ed was leaving right away, he could have his breakfast. *Result!*

But Ed was already reaching for it. "Yeah." He

regarded Clarissa, his spoon in the air. "Tell me about this kid you met at Groggs."

"Why?" Clarissa asked, looking suspicious.

"You said he was the manager?"

"Yes."

"He told you that?"

"Yes. I mean, I didn't believe it at the time, given he was so young. He had staff working there who were twice his age, but maybe he was a university graduate or something on one of their training programmes. He didn't seem old enough, though."

"And what did he look like?" Ed had yet to start on his cornflakes. Toby sat nicely and waited for the inevitable.

"Erm ... nineteen or twenty. A little taller than me. A kind of burnt orange hair. Acne. Blue eyes, I think. Not sure ..." She trailed off, watching Ed's change of expression. "What's up?"

"I don't know what to say really." Ed sank his spoon into his bowl of cereal. "I'm afraid ... I think you might be right."

"Right about what?"

"Not right about you being to blame, but right that there's a link."

"You're making zero sense, Ed," Toby said.

"What do you mean?" Clarissa asked, ignoring

the fact that Ed had started shovelling cornflakes into his gob as though his grandmother was about to appear and whisk the bowl away so she could wash it up.

Toby huffed with impatience. "Spit it out." He reconsidered this. "But not on the rug."

Ed swallowed and placed his bowl precariously on the edge of the sofa. Toby kept an eye on it for him.

"A call came in this morning. A woman found her son dead first thing. He worked for Groggs and his description matches the one you gave me."

"Oh no!" Clarissa slammed her bowl of cornflakes onto the coffee table, so hard that milk and flakes exploded everywhere.

"Obviously it isn't confirmed yet, so don't get upset," Ed told her.

"Don't get upset?" Clarissa shrilled. "Dee Dee, the mayor, Cathy and this poor kid—"

Oh yeah? Toby gave Clarissa a little side-eye. *Poor kid now, is it?* Not Harry Terribly Unhelpful now that he was a dead Groggs manager ...

"There may not be any link between them." Ed shifted uncomfortably. His bowl teetered. "It might just be a coincidence."

"If you believe that, you're not the detective I

think you are," Toby said, his tone grave. "And may I draw attention to your breakfast?"

"Your bowl, Ed!" Clarissa leaned forward and grabbed it before it could fall but too late to save the milk slopping. Toby diligently set about cleaning up. A dog's work is never done.

"Sorry," said Ed.

"It's fine." Clarissa placed Ed's bowl next to her own. "You have checked on Bryn, haven't you?"

"From Bryn's Bakes. Yes. Don't worry. We had someone go over there soon after I spoke to you this morning." He stood and reached for his jacket. "I'll check this out and then get back to you. If it *is* the manager of Groggs, I'll catch up with you a bit later. Will you be here?"

Clarissa hesitated. "I was going out. Call me on my mobile."

"Okay, will do."

"And if they do allow you to grab some sleep, you're welcome to come here."

"Thanks."

"I'll leave the back door open."

"You shouldn't do that," Ed said.

"It's Sun Valley. It's as safe as can be here."

"Unless you're a baker, apparently," said Ed.

Neither Clarissa nor Toby could disagree.

CHAPTER SEVENTEEN

"Are we sure this is a good idea?" Toby asked, staring up at the sign above the shop window. *Scrumpy Dumpy's. What sort of a name is that?*

"To be honest, I don't know whether it's a good idea or a bad idea," Clarissa admitted. "But I did promise myself that I'd check out all of the bakeries and, besides the one in the supermarket, this is the last one."

"There's one in the supermarket?" Toby couldn't picture this. He'd never been inside a supermarket. Dogs weren't allowed, apparently. This seemed ridiculously short-sighted to him. If dogs weren't allowed, how could they pressurise their owners into buying loads of snacks? Whenever Clarissa did the 'big shop' she came home with cans of food and a big bag of dog mix—but she rarely, if ever, bought anything more interesting than bone-shaped biscuits. If he'd been with her, he would have tried every dog treat in the store and probably the cat ones too.

"Haven't you ever been in a supermarket?" Sal asked, hanging out of Clarissa's pocket. She hurriedly pushed him back in.

"I've been inside the minimarket," Toby said. That's where he'd had to steal Sal's Hobnobs and his kweesh from, after their first meeting.

"Have you?" Clarissa gave him a sideways look.

"Erm ..." Toby coughed. "No. You're right. I haven't. I have no idea what the inside of any market looks like. Unless it's *the* market. The outdoor market with the burger van. I have absolutely no idea about mini or super or medium or mega or titanic markets."

"Hmm." Clarissa didn't sound convinced. "Yes, the supermarket has a bakery. They like to pretend it's an old-fashioned street," Clarissa told him. "Kind of cute but slightly weird," she said. "It's a bit like playing 'let's pretend' ..."

She turned away from Toby in order to take a couple of photos of Scrumpy Dumpy's just as a delivery van drew up in front of it. "Blast."

"It smells good," said Toby, inhaling the air. "Kind of meaty."

"That's because this bakery specialises in pasties and pies."

"Cor," said Sal, who was a sucker for a pie.

Come to that, so was Toby. "Wowsers," he said. "Any chance we could have one for lunch?"

"You've just eaten two bowls of cornflakes," Clarissa chided.

"Whaddayamean you had two bowls?" Sal asked Toby, completely scandalised. "I literally had a handful of dog biscuits."

"That was hours ago," Toby whined, evading Sal's query. "Go on! You know you'd love one yourself."

This wasn't strictly true. Clarissa was not a massive meat lover. "Maybe," she said. "We'll see."

We'll see. Toby wrinkled his nose in disgust. In his experience, 'we'll see' was one of those phrases used to pacify people. And dogs. Meaningless.

At that moment, the delivery van moved away and Clarissa began to take snaps.

Scrumpy Dumpy's had an attractive storefront. A gold canopy stretched over the bright white paint-work of the shop, and wooden pasties with cheerful smiles were used as decoration on either side of the window. In the window itself, Toby could see baskets of wares. Not just the semi-circular Cornish pasties, but also the ones with the crimped tops, plus a load of different pies and—much to Sal's delight—a variety of big kweeshes and mini kweeshes.

"Ride 'em, cowboy," Sal said, punching the air with his tiny fist. "Let's get over there and check out those bad boys!"

"It's a pie paradise," said Clarissa and, after looking both ways, crossed the road to stand under the canopy and ogle all the goodies on display. As she watched, Toby on his hind legs so he too could see, a woman in a red checked apron reached into the window and took out a couple of pies.

"Homity pies!" Clarissa breathed audibly. "Oooh. I haven't tried one of those for years."

"What's a homity pie?" Toby asked.

"Potato, leek, cheese—"

"Beef?" Toby asked.

"Only vegetables—"

"Ugh." Toby poked his tongue out. "What sort of a pie is that?"

"The sort that Clarissa likes," said Clarissa. "I may buy myself one and you can have some pastry crust."

"Oh, man," Toby complained, "that is not a good deal."

"And yet it may be the only deal on the table," Clarissa told him. "Like it or lump it."

An older gentleman standing at the door—the inside of the shop was jam-packed—gave Clarissa a sharp look. "Me?" he asked.

Clarissa flushed. "No, sorry. Beg your pardon. I was talking to my dog."

"He understands you, does he?"

"He does as it happens," Clarissa said.

The man laughed and tapped the side of his head. "The younger generation, eh?" He shot a look designed to elicit agreement from the woman standing behind him. The woman nodded but offered Clarissa a sympathetic look.

"I'm sure they understand far more than we know," she said.

"I'm sure I know far more than you understand," Toby said. *Pffffft!*

"Hush," said Clarissa and smiled at the woman gratefully. "Come on," she said to Toby.

Toby glared at the older man for one last time. *Buffoon!* "Where are we going?" he asked, resisting Clarissa's attempts to cross the road. "I thought we were buying a pie!"

"Our primary reason for being here is to speak to the owner of the bakery, not to buy pies!" Clarissa reminded him.

"But the pie is, like, a by-product, right?" Sal asked. He wasn't averse to sharing Clarissa's pie crust, especially if, as she'd said, it was *cheesy*!

"There's a bench over here. Let's sit on it and ..." She stared down at Toby's disappointed face. "We'll stake out the bakery. See who's coming and going. You never know, we might see the poisoner."

Toby liked the idea of staking. He preferred the idea of steak, but in the absence of steak, undertaking good old-fashioned detective work sounded fun to him. He hopped on the bench beside Clarissa and placed one paw on her thigh. "It might be worth taking some photos," he said.

"I'd start with taking some of that old-timer," Sal agreed. "What an old grouch he was."

Toby nodded. "That's true. Never trust anyone who doesn't like dogs."

"But we said that about Cathy." Clarissa lifted her camera to her eye.

"And look what happened to her!" Toby reminded her.

"At the time we weren't trusting her because we

thought she'd poisoned the mayor. Turns out that wasn't the case."

"Oh yes, that's true." Toby stared at the entrance to Scrumpy Dumpy's, trying not to be distracted by the heavenly aromas or the pie display. It was difficult to concentrate though.

"I reckon it's her," said Sal as an elderly lady, almost bent double and pulling a shopping bag on wheels, joined the back of the queue.

Toby studied the woman carefully. Maybe Sal could see something he couldn't. Was she in disguise? "Nope, can't see it myself," he said.

"Can't you?" Sal asked. "That's a shame."

"Why do you suspect her? She looks harmless to me."

"It's always the harmless ones you've gotta look out for. You should know that, mate." Sal folded his arms, looking smug.

Toby took another look. The old dear was pale with a pinky-peach-coloured lipstick. Her hair, apparently newly coiffed, was tucked under a white sunhat. She had swollen knuckles. They looked painful. Toby's heart went out to her.

"What are you on about, Sal?" Toby asked. "She can barely pull that trolley of hers."

"The trolley is where she keeps her poison," Sal said.

"What's he saying?" Clarissa asked.

"He reckons that old lady there with the sun bonnet is the poisoner."

"Does he?" Clarissa couldn't have sounded more scathing.

"I don't really," Sal said, rapidly backtracking. "I was just lettin' me imagination run free in the vain hope I was right and we could all buy a pie and go home."

"Good plan," said Toby, "and much appreciated. But could we at least try to find the real culprit?"

"Thing is, I don't suppose the actual poisoner is queuing up for a homity pie, do you?" Clarissa asked and put her camera to her eye again. She sometimes used it like binoculars because you could zoom in and see things more clearly.

"What if the two new victims are a distraction?" Sal asked.

Toby's ears twitched. "What?"

"Well, look at it this waaaaaaay." Sal drew the word out, thinking as he spoke. "What if ... right? Dee Dee was the *intended* victim but the mayor got in the way."

"Mmmm?"

"And to cover his or her tracks, the murderer decided to finish someone else off too?"

"Mmm." Toby wasn't sure he agreed with this theory. "But equally it might have been aimed at the mayor, and then when the mayor died, the murderer decided to cover his or her tracks by starting on the bakers."

Clarissa was listening with half an ear. She could follow Toby's line of argument but had to guess at Sal's. "What if it's some random who's watching me and murdering everyone I interview?" she asked.

Toby harrumphed. "Until we can figure out a motive, we'll never find the killer. And if we don't even know who the genuine victims are, then how can we come up with a motive?"

"It doesn't matter whether the victims are the intended ones or not," Clarissa told him. "They're all victims, and the killer must be brought to justice." She did a double take and turned to Toby, her camera in her lap. "But what am I even saying? I'm here to write an article, not play at detectives—"

"I'm not playing at being a detective! I *am* a detective!" Toby told her. "WPDCD Silverwind!"

"What is this WDDBD thing?"

"WPDCD. Wizarding Private Detective, Canine Division—"

"Oh, of course!" Clarissa rolled her eyes. "I remember."

"It's what I am," Toby told her primly. "So I suggest you ask questions and write words and leave the solving of murders to me. Deal?"

"Good grief," Clarissa muttered. "How do I get myself into these situations?"

"And another thing," said Sal. "We deserve payment for acting as your personal bodyguards. Payment in kind is acceptable. So about these pies ..."

CHAPTER EIGHTEEN

"I'm Clarissa Page, a journalist with *The Celestine Times* in London. Are you the owner?"

It was just after half past two, and finally the little bakery had quietened down enough for Clarissa to risk taking a chance on talking to the owner.

"I'm Mrs Scrumpy Dumps, yes." The woman seemed amused by this. She was probably amused by everything. Pink of chubby cheek and sparkling of eye, she appeared to have been blessed as one of life's great optimists.

"That's not your real name, is it?" Clarissa asked, her head on one side, clearly unsure whether the woman was pulling her leg or not.

Mrs Scrumpy Dumps snorted. "No, maid. My real name's Melissa Dumps, Harris as was, Liss as is, but ever since I married Mr Dumps, I've been known as Mrs Scrumpy Dumps or Old Liss. Scrumpy was my husband's nickname because he was fond of a pint or two of cider. Or a pint or six, I should say. The more he drank, the merrier he became. Bless him."

"Mr Dumps—"

"Passed away six years ago," Mrs Dumps said. "Much missed." She wiped her hands on her apron. "How can I help you, maid?"

Clarissa took a breath. Time to unleash the spiel about an article investigating competition between local businesses. She opened her mouth but the words wouldn't come out. She tried again. "I'm—" Nothing.

"Are you alright, sweet? You look a bit pale. Here, Henny!" Mrs Dumps turned to a woman sweeping the floor behind her. "Grab me a stool, will you?"

Sliding out from behind the counter, she regarded Clarissa with concern. "Almost grey, you are."

Henny, a middle-aged woman with a large waist and thick ankles, a pleasant face and kind eyes and an equally cheerful countenance, reappeared with a battered stool and handed it to Mrs Dumps. She guided Clarissa to it by the elbow and sat her down. "If you think you're going to faint, put your head between your knees."

"I'm fine," Clarissa protested, but she remained on the stool anyway, casting a sideways glance towards Toby hovering in the doorway to make sure he was remaining outside.

He was, of course.

On. Pain. Of. Death.

Or on pain of a lack of pie crust, which was even worse than death.

"You're probably low on sugar," Mrs Dumps decided. "Henny? Make Clarissa a hot chocolate—"

"That's not necessary," Clarissa said.

"Nonsense. I saw you earlier. You've been sitting over there on that bench for over two hours! I didn't realise you wanted to talk to me or I'd have come out!"

"But—"

"And is that your dog?" Mrs Dumps asked. "Let him come in. It's fine. We're quiet now, and we don't mind dogs anyway, do we, Henny?"

"We love dogs," said Henny from behind the

counter, where she was pouring milk into a jug ready to steam on the coffee machine.

"That's kind of you, thank you." Clarissa motioned Toby inside and he came in, dragging the lead and wagging his tail winningly at Mrs Dumps and Henny. Every little helped, he found.

"What a charmer," Mrs Dumps said. "A smashing boy." She leaned over and rubbed his head. "Now tell me, Clarissa, what was it you wanted to ask me about?"

Clarissa mentally screwed up her article and threw it into an imaginary litter bin. "I take it you've heard about the murders over the past few days?"

Mrs Dumps' face changed, her eyes becoming more serious. She let go of Toby and stood up. "Of course," she said, her voice giving nothing away. "Lots of our customers have been unable to talk about anything else, and I suspect that the reason we've been so busy today is because Cathy's and Bryn's are closed."

Clarissa recalled that Bryn had said he loved Mrs Dumps—or Old Liss as he'd called her. "You know them well?" she asked. "Cathy and Bryn?"

Henny set off the steaming machine, and for a moment nothing could be said or heard.

Eventually, Mrs Dumps could answer. "I do. I

knew their mother well. Poor Alison. I watched the kids grow up."

"Why do you say poor Alison?" Clarissa asked.

"Her husband left her when the kids were young so she had to run three bakeries simultaneously. That was alright while her mother was alive, but after she'd gone, it was a lot for her. She had managers in two of them, but as it turned out she was swindled by both of them! I mean, that's not right, is it?"

"Swindled?"

"Both of them—separately—were stealing money from her. She couldn't work out why the books would never balance. Eventually she got the police involved and one of the managers went to prison, I think. Not sure about the other one."

"I see."

Henny was frantically stirring chocolate into the milk now.

"When the kids were old enough—but still young—late teens, I think, Alison gave each of them a bakery to run. They did well, all things considered, but Bryn was the more ambitious of the two. He kept popping off to places to 'learn about baking,' he claimed, but it was a pain for poor Alison because she had to cover him in his bakery, and she was already getting on by then."

"Interesting," said Clarissa, pleased that Mrs Dumps liked to gossip. There were two sides to every story, and now she'd heard Bryn's and Mrs Dumps'. It was a shame that Cathy hadn't let on about Bryn, then she'd have had three angles to look at.

"I know Bryn always had a hankering to take over the market bakery, but in the end I think Alison decided Cathy would make a better go of it. Bryn was never there."

"And lots of competition, I suppose."

"Not so much competition. There was a real downturn in the fortunes of the high street back in the noughties. The big supermarket opened and even our daily market suffered—and, as you probably know, it's been a fixture in Sun Valley for centuries."

Clarissa nodded. "A proper market town."

"Exactly. And now down to only four days a week." Mrs Dumps stood back as Henny presented Clarissa with a mug of hot chocolate topped with whipped cream and Cadbury's Flake shavings.

"Oh wow, thank you," Clarissa enthused, wrapping her hands around it.

"Very nice," said Toby. "Any chance of sharesies?"

"Shh," said Clarissa.

"Cathy was a hard worker," said Henny. "I'm sad we've lost her so soon. I'd like to go to her funeral."

"We both must! I think we'll have to close as a mark of respect," Mrs Dumps said. "For at least half a day. I'll get in touch with Bryn in a few days and see if he'd like us to help with the funeral supper."

"Can you think of anyone who would have wanted to hurt Cathy?" Clarissa asked.

Mrs Dumps searched Clarissa's face. "You sound like a police officer."

Clarissa laughed. "Too much *Inspector Morse*," she said, narrowing her eyes in Toby's direction.

"Best show on the box," Toby replied confidently. "Besides *Midsomer Murders*. You can't beat a bit of Barnaby ..."

"I don't see much daytime telly." Mrs Dumps shrugged. "Not sure I'm missing much." She frowned, thinking. "I don't have a clue who might have wanted to hurt her. I mean ... maybe someone who wants to buy the premises? There's a lot of construction going on over there at the moment."

"That's true," Clarissa acknowledged. "What about ..." She took a beat, wondering how Mrs Dumps would take the next question.

"What about Bryn?" Mrs Dumps asked it for her. "No. He's a bit of a rogue and an idiot at times.

Selfish, maybe. But he doesn't need Cathy's Cakes. Look how well Bryn's Bakes is doing."

"Not even as ... vengeance?" Clarissa grimaced.

Mrs Dumps laughed. "I can't see it myself. Once upon a time they were very close."

Clarissa nodded. She would have to trust Mrs Dumps on that. She changed the subject. "Did you know the manager of Groggs?"

Mrs Dumps frowned, shaking her head. "Who's she?"

"I'm sorry, I don't know his name," Clarissa said. "A young man."

"Harry Terribly Unhelpful," Toby interjected.

Henny flapped a hand at Mrs Dumps. "That's what I was telling you earlier, Liss. The Pike kid. Jake Pike, is it? Or is that his brother? I always get the two mixed up."

"Oh, is that what you were on about? Beg your pardon, Henny. I was trying to stuff jam into a couple of hundred doughnut bottoms."

Toby widened his eyes. *That gives me a whole new outlook on jam doughnuts ... Ewww. They have bottoms?*

Not that Toby was allowed doughnuts.

"I heard it from one of the delivery drivers this morning," Henny said. "He heard it from somewhere else. Then a couple of our customers confirmed it, so it must be public knowledge."

Jake Pike. Clarissa stored that piece of information for later. "Does it worry you that bakers are being targeted by someone?" Clarissa asked.

Mrs Dumps looked startled. "Targeted? Are they?"

"Cathy and Jake," Clarissa said. "And Dee Dee Adamus?" Now both Henny and Mrs Dumps stared blankly at Clarissa. "The owner of The Magick Muffin?"

"That's the new bakery," Henny reminded Mrs Dumps.

"Is she dead?"

Clarissa could see she was causing confusion everywhere. "No. She *is* under suspicion of murdering the mayor though."

"Oh yes." Mrs Dumps waved a hand. "I remember."

"It was only at the weekend," Toby remarked.

"Memory problems," Sal squeaked. "Not enough cheese."

Clarissa blew on her hot chocolate. "What I'm getting at, I suppose, is that perhaps all of these cases are linked."

"Do you think so?" Mrs Dumps turned to Henny. "We might be next, Hen!"

"Heaven forbid!" Henny chuckled.

Mrs Dumps patted Clarissa's arm. "I think you're worrying too much, but isn't that the media all over these days. Making a mountain out of a molehill."

"I don't—"

"Only one baker has died," Mrs Dumps pointed out. "Poor Cathy. With the best will in the world, you can't call the Pike lad a baker. It's not five minutes since he left school. He doesn't—didn't—know the first thing about bread. And as for Lulu—"

"Dee Dee," Henny clarified.

"Whoever, she obviously isn't dead. She may have killed someone else. And that's an entirely different kettle of fish."

Clarissa couldn't argue with this logic.

"Was the mayor definitely murdered then?" Henny asked. "I knew he was dead and that foul play was being investigated, but—"

Clarissa nodded. "Yes. The autopsy found poison in his system."

"Hmmm." Mrs Dumps folded her arms across her chest. "I know I shouldn't speak ill of the dead, but I always knew that man would come to a sticky end."

"Really?" Clarissa waited, hoping for some good gossip.

Henny nodded. "He gave me the willies."

Tell us more, telegraphed Toby.

But Mrs Dumps seemed oddly reluctant to say much else.

"A few people have said similar things to me," Clarissa told her in the hope of loosening the older woman's tongue.

"Not a nice man," Mrs Dumps said. "You should go and chat with Gapper at The Red Lion. He'll have a story to tell."

"Gapper?" Clarissa asked, still hoping for more.

"Yes, he's the landlord. Been there forty-odd years. There's nowt he doesn't know about the businesses round here. Go and bend his ear."

Clarissa nodded. "Thank you so much for your time," she said and lifted her now empty mug. Henny took it from her. "And for your kindness. I feel better now."

"I don't," said Toby. "I feel faint with hunger!"

Clarissa tutted. "Would it be possible to buy a couple of pies?"

"Of course," said Henny, bustling around behind the counter. "What would you like?"

"Maybe ..." Clarissa looked at Toby, who watched her hopefully. "Steak?"

"That would be nice," he said.

"Steak and kidney?"

"That sounds offal," he said, and Sal squealed with laughter.

"A steak pie please." Clarissa smiled at Henny.

"No, I like offal," Toby interspersed.

Clarissa tutted. "Too late, furball."

Henny frowned at Clarissa.

"My dog," Clarissa said. "He's ... erm ... giving me cheek."

"One steak pie," said Henny, pulling it out of a basket in the window and wrapping it in a brown bag. "Anything else for you?"

"And a homity pie, please," said Clarissa and reached for her purse.

"On the house, maid," Mrs Dumps said. "I enjoyed the little walk down memory lane."

"Oh, I couldn't—"

"Of course you can," insisted Mrs Dumps. "Besides, we're getting to the end of the day and we always discount our bakes for a quick sale. You'll be doing me a favour."

A shadow fell across the door and all three women turned to the new arrival.

Clarissa recognised him straight away. Roddy Higwell. The journalist from the *Sun Valley Tribune*. He paid no attention to Clarissa—perhaps he didn't recognise her—he simply bustled into the shop. "Good afternoon, ladies!" he trilled. "How are you doing this fine day?"

The man was as fake as a Madam Tussaud's dummy. If he'd been made of wax, he'd have melted in the heat of the ovens.

Mrs Dumps smiled at Roddy. "What can I do for you, young man?" she asked.

Clarissa began to back out of the shop. "I'll be off. Thanks again," she said, waving to both women.

"Take care, maid!" Mrs Dumps called as Clarissa burst through the door and back into the fresh air, clutching her pies.

She took a moment to acclimatise, moving out of the way of a young woman and her pushchair before carefully placing the pies inside her bag on top of her camera. "I wonder what Roddy wants," she muttered.

"Is it lunchtime now?" Toby asked.

"Not yet," said Clarissa, despite it being after three. "I thought we'd visit the pub first."

CHAPTER NINETEEN

The Red Lion was a gorgeous old pub around the corner from Scrumpy Dumpy's. Mid-Victorian at a guess, it still had that olde-worlde charm that many pubs of that era had now lost. The bars—there were two, public and lounge—had fabulous old counters, highly polished and slightly worn. In the public bar there was a pool table, an old-fashioned jukebox and some battered tables and chairs. The lounge was a little more upmarket with better tables and chairs, but as dogs weren't allowed inside, Clarissa had to go into the public bar and sit on a tall stool at the counter.

"Not another stool," she mumbled. "My backside is killing me."

"How're you doing?" A young woman clutching a bar cloth approached Clarissa on the other side of the counter.

"Good, thanks," said Clarissa. "Is it possible to speak to Gaffer?"

"Gapper, you mean?" the woman asked.

"Oops, yes, sorry!"

"Sure. He's down in the cellar. I'll give him a shout." She walked half a dozen paces, opened a door and yelled down, "Gapper? Someone to see you!" before closing the door and returning to Clarissa. "Can I get you a drink?"

To Clarissa's mind it was a little early to start drinking—although there were plenty of people in the pub already doing so—but she felt the need to show willing and so ordered half a pint of cider. By the time the woman had poured it and taken Clarissa's money, a stocky older fellow with sparse white hair, a handlebar moustache and wearing a red lumberjack shirt had climbed up the stairs. He wiped his hands on a towel and approached Clarissa.

"Were you looking for me?" he asked.

"Mrs Scrumpy Dumps sent me over this way," Clarissa explained, and the man's face lit up. "Bless our Liss. One of my favourite people," he said. "What did she think I could do for you?"

"My name's Clarissa Page," Clarissa said. "I'm a journalist with *The Celestine Times* in London."

"Page is a good name for a journalist, isn't it?" Gapper asked.

Sharp as a tack, this one, thought Toby.

Clarissa laughed, as though she hadn't heard that comment over a zillion times before. "It's the name I was born with."

Gapper nodded. "You have a look of someone I used to know."

Clarissa's heart missed a beat. It might have been her mother or father, neither of whom she'd known for very long, or ... "My grandfather was Joseph Silverwind."

"Joe Silverwind. That's it! You do have a look of that old geezer about you. A truly lovely gentleman."

Clarissa felt oddly touched. "Thank you," she said. "That means a lot to me."

"To us," said Toby, at her feet.

"To us," Clarissa agreed. "I inherited Toby after he passed away."

Gapper peered over the bar. "Hello, handsome," he said.

"Back atcha," said Toby, already liking this landlord a great deal.

"So you wanted to ask me about ...?" Gapper

raised his eyebrows, reached for a half-pint glass and poured himself a short measure of stout.

Clarissa lowered her voice and took a quick look around. "Mayor Casterford."

"Ah." Gapper drank off the stout and poured himself a little more. "No wonder Liss sent you to me."

"Do you mind talking about it?" Clarissa asked.

"No, not at all." Gapper grinned. "The man was corrupt to the core. It always surprised me he was never charged with fraud or something. He did do some jail time in the past, but not enough to mar his chances of becoming mayor, unfortunately."

"He went to prison?" Clarissa leaned forward, intrigued. "Tell me about him."

"Hmm. He first came to my attention when he was in his early twenties, I suppose. A bit of a spiv, he was. I'd been landlord here five or six years by then probably. I caught him dealing in stolen goods from the gents out the back, so I turfed him out and barred him. Then a few years later he showed up again, in a suit, claiming he was from the council."

Gapper sneered. Clarissa laughed at Gapper's expression.

"I didn't believe a bloody word of it. Thought he

was pulling my leg. So I reminded him—politely—that he was barred and kicked him out again."

"And?" Clarissa was invested now.

"Next thing I know I was getting a phone call from his boss *at the council*. Turns out they *had* employed him and they'd put him in the licensing and permits section. I was howling!" Gapper hooted. "Imagine that! Imagine *anyone* employing that idiot. I says to the woman on the phone, I says, 'Well, I don't want nothing to do with him, so if you need me to sign anything or fill in your forms, you'll have to come and see me yourself.'"

"And did she?"

"She did, as it happens. Nice lady. Always polite. Knowledgeable. You know. The problem was she retired three or four years later, and guess who ended up in charge?"

"Not Casterford, surely?" Even Clarissa felt outraged, and she'd hardly known the man.

"Yep. So after that I had no bleeding choice, did I? If I wanted licences and permits for events and late-night opening and what have you, I had to have dealings with him."

"How did that go?"

"About as you'd expect. The trouble with Casterford is he made a lot of noise, but he didn't know his arse from his elbow, quite frankly."

"Oh dear."

"Yeah. Forms would get lost or he'd swear something was in the post but it wasn't, and so on and so forth." Gapper poured himself a little more stout. "Then he got in trouble with the bookies. Owed them money, I think. That's what I heard. And he started leaning on us mere mortals."

"Landlords?"

"Pretty much anyone who needed a licence, a permit, fire and safety certificates, rate exemptions … you name it, he had his finger in every pie. That affected an awful lot of businesses in Sun Valley. Not just pubs, but the bakers, the butchers, garages, hair salons, chemists, everyone who had a stake in the town."

Stake. Steak. Oh. Toby's stomach rumbled. He could smell the pie in Clarissa's bag. It was calling to him. *Tobeeeee! Tobeeeeeeeeeee!*

"What exactly did he do?"

"He would demand money with menaces."

Clarissa's chin jutted out. "What?"

"Not menaces as in he was going to bring the boys around and smash the place up, not like that. He'd just put pressure on us to 'donate' to him in order for him to oversee the greasing of the wheels and the oiling of the cogs. If you agreed, that would get your permit signed or your request for an extension granted."

"I see." Clarissa whistled. "Didn't people complain?"

"I think lots of business owners felt intimidated. For some of the bigger ones, twenty quid here or there was never going to break the bank—"

"But it's the principle of it," said Clarissa, outraged on behalf of the business community.

Gapper laughed. "Casterford *never* had any principles."

"Did he ever get caught?"

"He did. I lost count of how many times I protested to the council, but in the end I organised a petition and we delivered it to the then mayor, who took it upon himself to make sure Casterford was fired."

"Good."

"He was investigated. That's when he did a couple of years inside for fraud or something. When he came out he was quiet for a long time. Didn't hear a peep out of him, and then a couple of years ago he decided to make a bid for mayor."

"And he won?" Clarissa asked, hardly able to believe it.

"Sun Valley folk have short memories, I swear. Particularly the ladies, if you don't mind me saying so."

Clarissa *did* mind the insinuation, but that's the thing about asking people questions when you're interviewing them for an article. You can't let your own emotions get in the way of the story. "Why women?" she asked, keeping her tone neutral.

"Cos he could charm them. Especially the older ones. Yeah, he was beloved by the blue rinse brigade. Lots of them donated to his campaign." Gapper chuckled. "Not many of us business owners did though."

Clarissa harrumphed. "I'm not surprised."

"Course, as soon as he took office, he was straight back to it. Backhanders, favours under the counter."

"Did you complain?"

"Who to?" Gapper asked. "Even the leader of the local council couldn't keep Casterford in check. I think everyone gave up. Left him to it."

"Did you try involving the police?"

Gapper shrugged. "They said it was a civil matter."

"That must have driven you mad."

"It did." Gapper drained his glass. "I'll tell you something for nothing, whoever knocked off Casterford did the whole town a favour!"

CHAPTER TWENTY

Clarissa slept like the dead.

Fortunately ***not*** *the dead, though,* thought Toby when he came in to check on her the following morning. He supposed this was a result of the previous night's lack of sleep. She lay on her side, her eyes covered by a sleep mask which bore the immortal words *Rest in Peace and Quiet*, and snored gently.

Toby prodded her.

"Mmm," she mumbled, then resumed snoring again.

"Is there any chance of breakfast?" Toby asked, thoughts of yesterday's pie warming the cockles of his heart. If only he could have a pie for breakfast too. If only they lived next door to Scrumpy

Dumpy's. *Hey! Maybe we can move? I'll put that to Clarissa and see what she says!*

He was about to paw her again when her mobile—in its usual place on her bedside table—began warbling.

"Wah!" Clarissa sat upright, knocking Toby off the bed as she reached for her phone with one hand and tried to remove the eye mask with the other.

"What time is it?" she asked, her voice husky.

The high-pitched warble on the other end told Toby—trying to recapture some of his lost dignity and find a space where he could jump back up on the bed—that this was Rowena, Clarissa's boss.

"No." Clarissa rubbed her face. "No. I've literally just woken up." She listened some more then added, "No. I don't get the local paper delivered. Why would I? They fired me!"

Oh dear. Toby peered up at Clarissa, who was looking peeved. This conversation was evidently not going well.

"Roddy wrote that?" Clarissa asked. "Aha." She winced as Rowena's voice became ever higher and louder. "I appreciate that, but I can't just pick any angle willy-nilly and run with it. I think we have a duty to report the situation accurately, and at the moment—"

Rowena interrupted her. Clarissa listened impatiently and then finally picked her moment to speak up. "At the moment—" she repeated, her voice raised, "I don't understand what the situation is. Rowena, please listen to me!" Clarissa sounded a little desperate. "Of course, *you* can fire me too, but I am working hell for leather on this story, and I'm happy to sub something but I haven't drawn any conclusions yet. It's a story in progress! I don't know what else to tell you."

Perhaps Rowena had calmed down a little because Toby couldn't hear her now. Clarissa listened, nodding, occasionally adding 'yes' or 'of course' until finally, more calmly, she said, "I *have* never and *will* never make up a story or sensationalise what I know. If that's what you want, then you'd be better off contracting Roddy. In the meantime, I'll carry on doing all the research I need and I'll report the facts. I will sub you something later today, but it won't be whatever rubbish Roddy is spouting."

Rowena said something else and Clarissa's answer was curt. "Absolutely. Speak later." She hung up and threw back her quilt. "ARGH!"

"Everything alright?" Toby asked, taking a step backwards. He'd never seen Clarissa look so furious before. Well, not since the night he'd made the family-sized bottle of tomato ketchup mysteriously explode when he was practising some spells in the kitchen. The sauce had spattered everywhere, all over Toby and even on the ceiling, just as Clarissa had been on her way to bed.

Yes, she'd been pretty cross.

Or there was the time he'd made one of her precious notebooks disappear. He'd wanted to practise making things he vanished come back again. Like the bees ... *Hmm.* Unfortunately, no matter how many spells he cast, he wasn't able to get the notebook back.

Clarissa hadn't spoken to him *for hours!*

She'd been furious.

But not as enraged as she was now.

"That blasted Roddy! He went into Scrumpy Dumpy's after us yesterday, didn't he?"

"Yes," said Toby.

"I reckon he's been following me or ... or ... something because according to Rowena, the *Sun Valley Tribune* have published a full front-page story about how all the bakeries in Sun Valley are closing down thanks to a serial killer!"

"A cereal killer?"

"Yes! They've run with the story that a serial killer is stalking the bakers."

"Erm ..." Toby gawked up at Clarissa as she reached for the clothes she'd dumped over the bedstead the previous night. "That *is* one of our theories, isn't it?"

"That's not the point!" grumbled Clarissa. "We don't have any proof." She hauled on fresh underwear and yesterday's black gypsy skirt, sniffed yesterday's t-shirt, pulled a face and dropped it on the floor. "Smells of pie."

Yummy, thought Toby. *I could sleep on that. It would make for great dreams!*

Clarissa yanked open a drawer at the bottom of her wardrobe and flipped through the contents. Not much there. In desperation she scooped up yesterday's t-shirt and pulled it on regardless. "This'll have to do. We're only going to the newsagent's."

"Okay." Toby trotted along, deciding it would be best for him if he kept the peace rather than enquiring about the likelihood of Clarissa being fired from *The Celestine Times*. That would be bad news for both of them because the last time she'd been out of work, they hadn't even had enough money to buy bread for sammiches.

"Are we taking Sal?" Toby asked when they

arrived downstairs and Clarissa unlocked the front door.

"We'll be back in half an hour. Can't he amuse himself for that amount of time?" Clarissa asked.

Toby thought of all the ways Sal liked to amuse himself. For the most part they involved chewing something to bits or eating things he shouldn't or that didn't belong to him or both. "Probably," said Toby, casting a glance towards the kitchen.

"Good. Let's go."

Clarissa marched outside and down the path to the gate, jabbing her thumb towards the front door without looking. Toby hardly made it out in one piece before the door slammed. He turned to stare at it in surprise. Clarissa had magicked it shut and he'd nearly lost the tip of his tail.

"Erm—"

"Hurry up, Toby, or I'll leave you here!"

Wowsers. "It's just—"

"Come on!"

Clarissa had turned down Chamberlain Drive now. Toby hurried after her, almost missing Moriarty's greeting.

"Good morning," she purred.

Toby paused. "I can't stop," he said.

Moriarty sympathised. "Trouble with the hooman?"

"She's a woman possessed this morning! Gotta go!"

"Good luck," Moriarty said. "Seems like the whole of Sun Valley is revolting this morning."

"I wouldn't say Clarissa is revolting," said Toby, "just ... a bit touchy at times." With that, he took to his paws and raced after Clarissa, who was steaming ahead.

"You forgot your—" Moriarty called after him, but Toby was already out of earshot.

The walk into town was usually undertaken at a moderate pace and took ten to twelve minutes. Today they did it in seven, which was pretty good considering Clarissa didn't even break into a sweat. She kept up a regimented stride, looking neither right nor left, and swung her arms like a soldier on parade.

Progress was halted rather unexpectedly, however, as they turned down Mayflower Lane, making a beeline for the marketplace. Toby wasn't exactly sure why she'd walked this far, given that the minimarket was closer to their house and it sold newspapers.

But perhaps it was journalistic instinct because,

as they reached the junction with the marketplace, Toby became aware of some kind of ruckus.

At first he thought it was a fight, although why people would be fighting on a Wednesday morning in the middle of the town, he had no idea. All of the fights he'd ever seen—on the telly, naturally—happened outside pubs at closing time. "I'm not sure this is a good idea," he barked as Clarissa elected to charge forwards. "I'm sure Ed wouldn't like us doing this!"

Whether Clarissa heard him or not, Toby had no clue, but she had slowed down and now, halfway along Mayflower Lane, just after Sweet Pea's Parlour for Pampered Pooches, she ground to a halt.

"What is it?" Toby asked, pausing alongside her.

"People," said Clarissa, although this was obvious. "Carrying placards. Look!"

"What are placards?" Toby asked, following her finger to where it pointed.

"See? They're carrying signs? With writing on. Those are placards. It must be some kind of protest."

This was a new one on Toby. *A protest?*

"Come on." Clarissa started forward and then stopped. "Blast! I forgot my camera." She patted her pockets. "I do have my phone though. Let's go."

She broke into a run, almost a sprint, Toby

chasing after her. Once they reached the end of the lane, Clarissa slowed down, breathing heavily, and aimed her mobile at the crowd, snapping photos.

Toby stared up at all the people, trying to read the signs, which wasn't easy given that the crowd were milling around and shouting and generally being more animated than Toby was used to on a Wednesday morning in Sun Valley's sleepy marketplace.

"Two, four, six, eight. What do we appreciate?" a woman with a megaphone demanded to know.

"Cake!" everyone else shouted back.

"What?" Clarissa moved her phone down so she could see better. "What are they chanting?"

"Two, four, six, eight!" the crowd roared. "What do we appreciate? Cake!"

"Did they say cake?" Clarissa asked.

"They did," Toby confirmed.

"Why are people protesting about ... cake?"

"Let's find out," Toby suggested and trotted out among the crowd.

"Come back!" Clarissa belatedly realised Toby had no lead. But Toby was away, intent on finding out what was going on. He darted among people's ankles until he reached the other side of the line. From his new vantage point, he realised that the march wasn't as mahoosive as it looked. It wound around the marketplace so that the front of the march almost met the back of it, rather like a roundabout ride.

Clarissa fought her way through the crowd, apologising to the people she had to push aside as she did so, until she was able to join Toby on the other side. She reached down and made a grab for his collar but Toby skipped sideways, having none of it. Realising keeping hold of him would be untenable for any length of time, she wagged a finger at him. "You stay within five feet of me or I'll lock you up in the bathroom for three weeks."

Toby tittered. "What happens when you get caught short, then?"

"I'm warning you, fuzzball!"

"Okay, okay!"

Satisfied, Clarissa lifted her mobile again and began recording a video, homing in on the placards.

Save are bakries! said one.

Our bakers are a precious commodity! claimed a second.

At least someone stayed awake in English class, thought Clarissa.

Let us eat cake!!! roared another sign, complete

with a drawing of Marie Antoinette—or someone who resembled her. Clarissa rather liked that one.

"Excuse me?" Clarissa caught the attention of a woman who had stopped to fix her own placard, which had become floppy. "Can you tell me what's going on here?"

"Haven't you heard about the dead bakers?" the woman asked.

"Yes ..."

"There's a conspiracy to shut all the bakeries in Sun Valley," the woman said. "Four bakeries are closed—"

"Four?"

"That new one—"

"The Magick Muffin?"

"That's the one. Plus Cathy's, Bryn's and now Groggs."

"Groggs is closed?" This was a new one on Clarissa.

"Yep!" The woman shook her head. "A load of customers went down with food poisoning over the past few days, and the outbreak has been traced to Groggs."

"I didn't know that!"

"It's true. I don't know whether it's linked to their baker who died—"

"Harry Terribly Unhelpful," said Toby.

The woman glanced down at Toby. "But I wouldn't be surprised."

"It is all a bit odd," Clarissa agreed.

"And we want to know why the police aren't doing anything about it."

Clarissa debated whether to respond to this or not. She knew how hard Ed had been working; he hadn't had more than a few hours' sleep at a time over the past few days. "Why are you protesting here?" Clarissa asked. "You could protest at the police station."

"We figured this would be more public, right in the heart of the town. It's a tribute to Cathy—" The woman pointed in the direction of Cathy's Cakes, the shop shuttered and dark. "It will also cause the most disruption because the traffic can't get around us." The woman grinned with glee. "It was Roddy's idea—"

"Roddy? Roddy as in Roddy Higwell? The reporter?"

"Yes. Brilliant, isn't it?"

"It certainly is," Clarissa said, watching as the woman gave up on her placard, folded it up and made a beeline for a rubbish bin.

"Is that rotten Roddy here anywhere?" she asked

Toby. "Can you see him?"

"I can smell him," Toby said. "Over there." He set off across the market and Clarissa hurried to follow him.

"What do we want?" a man with a megaphone yelled.

"Cake!" roared the marchers.

"When do we want it?"

"Now!"

"How do we want it?"

"Baked by live bakers!"

"Extraordinary," muttered Clarissa. By no means did she have a problem with the message, not at all—it was only that she'd never attended or heard of such a protest before.

Certainly, the commotion had attracted the police because a pair of panda cars had turned up and four apprehensive coppers were climbing out of them, zipping up jackets and adjusting earpieces.

And there was Roddy, wearing earphones and carrying a massive microphone with a furry cover. Beside him, one of the *Sun Valley Tribune* photographers was busy taking photos of the marchers, zooming in on angry faces or zooming out to get shots of the hordes.

Clarissa sidled up to Roddy. "What's all this?"

she asked.

Roddy turned, saw who it was and curled his lip. Toby growled at him and Roddy took a step back. "What does it look like?" he said, half an eye on Toby.

"I just spoke to a woman in the crowd who said this was all your idea!"

Roddy's face turned smug. "It might have been. Some of it."

"You're supposed to write about the news, not make it happen!" Clarissa couldn't hide her disgust.

"Over the past few days I've been speaking to many of the locals here," Roddy told her, his nose in the air. "And they've been confiding their concerns about the dead bakers and that they think there's a conspiracy afoot to close all of the remaining bakeries in town."

"Who would do that?" Clarissa asked, not hiding her scepticism. "Do you have any idea?"

Roddy feigned innocence. "You literally just told me I should report the news, not make it, so why would I have any idea?" He waved a hand. "However, some fine and upstanding members of the community fear that the people behind it are Sebco."

"Sebco?" Clarissa laughed, more in disbelief than anything else. "The supermarket?"

"The global supermarket chain? Yes."

"That's the most ridiculous thing I've ever heard," Clarissa told him. "Why would a supermarket chain target a couple of artisan bakers?"

"Not forgetting Jake Pike, of course. He wasn't an artisan, was he?"

"No. But—"

"I'm sure Sebco would like to see the back of Groggs—"

"Maybe. But—"

"Sebco's market share is down year on year, and their forecast for next year has been downgraded. Groggs are on the up. How better for a global brand to claw back consumers than eliminating the competition?"

"I don't buy it." Clarissa shook her head. "I really don't see how Cathy's Cakes made a dent in Sebco's profits. And who, in the almighty freezer aisle, is the person who would do the poisoning on behalf of Sebco? Have they hired a contract killer or have they asked Mavis off the checkouts?"

Roddy pursed his lips. "I don't think you're taking this seriously."

"I'm taking it incredibly seriously, but I'm not plucking fairy stories out of thin air and ascribing them to some fanatical local!"

"Whatever!" Roddy held up a hand in Clarissa's face. "I'll get on with my job and you can do yours for your fancy London newspaper."

"I will!"

"Good!" Roddy began to walk away.

"It's not ethical!" Clarissa called after him. "You're the sort of person who gives mainstream media a bad name! You're stirring up trouble!"

"I'm giving the people what they want!" Roddy yelled back before melting into the crowd.

Clarissa sighed, her heart thumping hard. "Yes," she muttered. "Giving the people an excuse to take to the streets and—"

A horn blasted close by. Someone screamed. Clarissa and Toby turned as one. A delivery van was attempting to get through from Mayflower Lane and do a left turn out of the market. Unfortunately, the crowd weren't prepared to give ground. The van tried to push through and a couple of people were knocked sideways.

"Oh, my goddess!" Clarissa lifted her mobile and began taking photos. "What does he think he's doing?"

"Someone's going to get hurt if they're not careful," Toby said.

"Stay close. I don't want you getting trampled."

"I don't want to *be* trampled!" Toby carefully picked his paws up, one by one, higher than they needed to be. He looked a little comical, and he certainly couldn't walk very quickly.

The van had been surrounded by angry protesters now, and a couple of them were bashing the windows and the sides of the vehicle with their placards. The police were moving in to push people back to safety and direct the van down the road, but the crowd were angry and out of control. People began throwing things—anything they could get their hands on, including the wares from nearby stalls.

In turn, the market traders came out fighting. "Oi!"

Clarissa grimaced. "Oh, it's all kicking off!"

Four police officers could not contain the ruckus. Clarissa climbed onto a bench so she had a better vantage point for taking photos. Toby climbed up beside her, not so that he could see, but more to protect his precious tootsies. Men were shouting, women were screaming, people were throwing saucepans and brooms, boxes of fudge and polyester sweaters.

"The world's gone crackers," said Toby.

"And all thanks to Roddy Higwell," grumbled Clarissa.

CHAPTER TWENTY-ONE

Clarissa snacked on a slice of honey on toast and pored over the *Sun Valley Tribune*.

Toby wasn't sure how he felt about honey. He liked the taste but was wary of upsetting his neighbourhood bees any more than he already had. He was the unforgiven one where bees were concerned.

However, toast corners, especially ones that had been properly spread with butter, were acceptable. And the good thing about Clarissa being so engaged in what she was reading was that she simply kept handing him the corners without really thinking about it.

"What Roddy said about Groggs is true," Clarissa noted. "There was an outbreak of food poisoning cases overnight on Monday into Tuesday. Three people went to hospital and scores more unwell."

"Monday is the day we talked to Groggs," Toby recalled.

"I'm glad we didn't buy anything from them," said Clarissa. "It says that the outbreak has been traced back there, although they've yet to discover whether it was confined to one specific product they sell."

"It might have been one of the ingredients," Toby said, reaching up for the next toast corner.

Clarissa handed it over. "But remember, they don't make their own products—the products come from a factory. They only have to bake them on site." She pulled out her notebook and wrote that down.

"That's right, you did say that," Toby agreed. "What do you think of this Sebco idea?"

"It's crazy." Clarissa dismissed it out of hand. "There's no way that a handful of local bakeries can affect a giant supermarket's bottom line to that extent."

"Okay. I'll take your word for it," Toby said, although he didn't have the foggiest what bottom lines and forecasts and year-on-year projections were. Clarissa spoke about them with ease, however, so he decided she probably knew what she was talking about.

"Can I turn the telly on?" Toby asked.

"No," said Clarissa. "I'm going to write up a story about the protest and increased tensions within the community after the recent spate of bakery-related deaths. And I, unlike a certain so-called journalist of our acquaintance, will not resort to stoking the fires of local sensibilities."

Toby decided it was time to withdraw. Clarissa had her wordsmith head on and it would be better for him if he didn't interrupt. He went in search of Sal instead and found his fat friend sunbathing on the ladder steps of the wizarding shed.

"What've you been up to this morning?" Toby asked him.

"This 'n' that," said Sal and absentmindedly patted his belly.

"Have you been eating something?"

"I may have raided Mrs Crouch's parlour." Sal tried his best to sound apologetic. He failed miserably.

Toby growled at Sal. "I thought I'd told you that Mrs Crouch is off limits!"

"Yeah, yeah, you did. I tried to resist, honest, but I didn't get no breakfast this morning and there's nuffink in our own pantry—"

"But Mrs Crouch is so good to us! You can't thieve from her!"

Sal performed a jerky dance. "If she's got it, I want it. If I want it, I've got it."

"You really can't help yourself?" Toby was disgusted.

"Nope."

"Tobes?" Clarissa appeared at the back door.

Obediently, he hurried over to see her, tail wagging.

"I need to nip out. The printer has run out of cyan ink and refuses to print. It's a royal pain! I only need black and white."

"I thought you were writing?" Toby asked, aware that Clarissa's sub deadline tended to be around four in the afternoon.

"I am. I will be. I can think of the wording I'm going to use while I'm out and I'll write it more quickly when I'm back. But if I don't get the ink now, I won't be able to print the article out and edit it."

Clarissa liked to do her editing the old-fashioned way, on paper with a red pen. It seemed like a waste of trees to Toby.

"I won't be long." Clarissa leaned down and kissed his head. "Behave."

"I always behave," Toby told her. "It's everyone else."

Toby waited until he heard Clarissa drive off—over-revving as usual—and snuck back into the house to check for stray toast corners or random snacks. He didn't find anything though. He'd done a perfectly wonderful job of clearing up earlier.

"Whoo-hoo! There's a whole slice of toast up here!" Somehow Sal had managed to clamber up onto Clarissa's dining table-come-desk and had located her plate and a triangle of buttered honey toast.

"Awww!" Toby couldn't believe his eyes. "Sharesies!"

"Haven't you eaten?" Sal leaned over the table and waved the toast like a football trophy.

"Barely," said Toby and jumped at the table leg to wobble it.

Two things happened in virtual slow motion. Firstly, Sal lost his balance and tumbled over the edge of the table, throwing the slice of toast into the air before plummeting towards Toby. Toby stared up in alarm, calculating the rate of descent for rat versus toast. What were the chances of Sal hurting himself on landing if Toby opted to catch the toast? Would the toast land butter side down if Toby caught Sal?

Secondly, and at the same time as Toby's brain tried to compute this, a pile of Clarissa's research—pushed close to the edge of the table in order to give her plate room while she was eating—also began to topple.

Toby manoeuvred himself to catch Sal in his mouth—an altogether scary prospect for the rat—at the expense of the toast quarter that splodged down beside them, butter side down naturally, just as the two creatures were showered in photos, sheets of paper, newspapers, pens and Post-its.

"Waaaaaaah!" Sal cried.

A book landed on Toby's head. *Thunk.*

"Ow!" he said and dropped Sal.

"Oof," said Sal, landing on his not inconsiderable rump.

Toby closed his eyes. "I have a headache."

Sal countered that. "I have a butt ache."

"I might have to have a lie-down for the rest of the afternoon," said Toby, flopping onto the floor.

Sal surveyed the wreckage scattered around them. "I'd join you, but I think one of us is gonna need to conduct a salvage operation ..."

Toby looked around. *Doggone it.*

Behave, Clarissa had said, and now look what they'd done. Toby sighed. "You're right. We'd better clear it up."

Sal started with the pens. This was no easy task as he could only manage one at a time. Toby opted to begin gathering the photographs. Rather than doghandle them with his mouth and risk getting them covered in schnauzer spit, he levitated each one individually and began to create a fresh pile in front of himself.

He'd collected together about twenty of the photos when something caught his eye. He cosied up to the image on top and stared down at it. Sal, huffing and puffing with a fluorescent marker, paused his own efforts. "What are you doing?" he complained. "You can't rest on the job. She'll be back in a minute to kick our butts, and my butt's already sore!"

"This man," Toby said, tapping the page. "I recognise him."

Sal dropped the fluorescent marker and sidled over to Toby. "Do you?"

Toby straightened the photo and examined it again. It was one Clarissa had taken this morning at the protest. It showed the cab of the van and the driver who had been attempting to manoeuvre his way through the noisy throng.

"It's not the best photo," Toby said. "It's a bit grainy. It looks like Clarissa tried to enlarge it."

"But you think you recognise this geezer?" Sal asked, stepping on the image.

Toby brushed him away. "I do. A delivery driver. Are there any more long shots of this morning?" He scattered the images he'd already collected then sifted through them. "Grab the rest of the photos, Sal."

Sal scampered around, gripping the eight-by-six photos in his teeny paws and dragging them over to Toby one by one. Toby scanned each new arrival, searching for the market-based images. "Here!" he cried excitedly. "This is a long shot of the van."

Sal came over to take a look. "What does it say on the side?"

Toby studied the van's markings and logo. There was a paper cup or mug—the kind you received your drink in when you went to a takeaway coffee shop—hand drawn and depicting a cheery, grinning face, filled with brown liquid, steam rising from the top. "It says Cooper and Company's Cup Dispensing Service."

"What's that mean?"

"I suppose Cooper is the name of the owner."

"But what's a cup dispensing service?"

Toby had a vague notion of what dispensing meant. "Kind of like giving out cups, I think."

Sal crooked his head to one side. "I reckon I've seen that van before, now you mention it. I recognise the smiling cup thing."

Toby nodded. "I suppose we see a lot of things when we're out and about."

"Yeah but no," said Sal, which confused Toby enormously.

"Huh?" Toby asked.

"I saw it yesterday, when we were waiting outside Scrumpy Dumpy's."

Toby thought back. That was a *lonnnnnng* time ago. He couldn't be sure the delivery van they'd seen then was the same as this one, but it was feasible. "It's a delivery van's job to deliver things," he reminded Sal. "We might have seen it anywhere."

"I know," said Sal, scratching his head. "So he was delivering cups to Scrumpy Dumpy's."

"A takeaway cup ..." Toby stared down at the image. "I wonder who else he delivers to?"

"Are you thinking what I'm thinking?" Sal asked.

"I'm not sure my thinking machine is thinking

particularly well," Toby admitted. "Not since that book hit me on the bonce!"

Sal gripped a pawful of Toby's fur. "It would be easy for a delivery driver to gain access to lots of businesses ..."

Toby nodded. "And most bakeries do takeaway coffee and tea." He peered around at the rest of the photos scattered across the floor. "Let's look through every single one of these and see if we can see him in any of the others!"

"On it!" Sal jumped around excitedly from photo to photo, but Toby was more diligent. He began to divide the images into sets. Lots of The Magick Muffin's opening afternoon. Loads from Scrumpy Dumpy's, and fewer of Groggs, Bryn's Bakes and Cathy's Cakes. But there were two photos that really stood out.

One, taken from in front of Scrumpy Dumpy's when the delivery van drove up, confirmed Sal's memory of seeing it before. The other was a surprise. It showed part of the rear of a van parked a little further down the road from Cathy's Cakes. Toby couldn't see the logo clearly, but the colours used matched the colours of Cooper and Company's Cup Dispensing Service livery.

"It doesn't prove anything," Toby said. "I'm sure

Inspector Barnaby would say it was circumstantial. We're probably grasping at straws."

They sat beside each other staring at the photos for some time.

Clarissa found them like that when she arrived home clutching a multipack of printer inks, a ream of A4 printer paper and a pack of printable photograph card. "What's going on here?" she asked, dropping the car keys and her battered old bag onto the table along with her new purchases. "What a mess!"

"We had a little accident," Toby said.

"I can see that!" Clarissa frowned and crouched down to begin scooping up the photos.

"Wait!" Toby stopped her. "We think there's something you might want to see."

The urgency in his voice stopped her. "Have you found something?"

"It might be something or nothing," Toby admitted. "And it was Sal who drew my attention to it. Sal the supersleuth."

"Shucks," said Sal, scuffing his back feet on the rug and flushing. "It was both of us."

"But see this van?" Toby pointed out the long-distance image of this morning.

"Mmm?" Clarissa plucked up the photo and

scowled at it. "That was the driver who tried to bully his way through the crowd."

"That's right." Toby indicated the second one outside Scrumpy Dumpy's.

"I took that yesterday while we were waiting," Clarissa said, picking it up and comparing it to the first. "It's the same van."

"Right. And then there's this one." Toby used his nose to push the one taken outside Cathy's Cakes on the day Clarissa interviewed her.

"Hmmm." Clarissa wiggled her head. "It could be the same van. It's difficult to tell."

"We were just wondering—Sal and I—whether the person behind all the bakery trouble could be a delivery driver?"

Clarissa sat back on her haunches, looking from one photo to the next and back again, taking her time, thinking. Finally she stood up.

"What do you think?" Toby asked.

"I don't know," Clarissa said. "But it occurs to me that I've taken hundreds of photos and only printed out dozens. I didn't want to waste paper. I think ..." Her voice trailed off as she sat at her laptop and began punching the keyboard, squinting at the screen.

Toby clambered up on the chair beside her, looking over her shoulder. She'd scrolled right back to the photos she'd taken of The Magick Muffin, and now she clicked past every image that didn't have a delivery van in it. In the case of The Magick Muffin, that was all of them.

Except ...

Hadn't a delivery driver held up proceedings while he delivered ... stuff?

Yes. Clarissa had a dim memory of that. What had he been delivering?

Another shuffle through the images didn't prove enlightening.

Sighing, Clarissa moved on to Cathy's Cakes, and this time she struck gold. A much clearer image of Cooper and Co's Cup Dispensing Service's delivery van.

Clarissa sat back. "None of this proves anything."

"We know," said Toby, glancing down at Sal who was staring up at them, nodding.

"But I do think it's worth drawing Ed's attention to it. In fact, he's due back on shift at seven, so I'll go over there and have a chat with him and show him the photos."

"Sounds like a plan," Toby said, pleased that

they'd managed to spawn some sort of lead, even if it amounted to nothing in the end.

"But first I have to get this article written for Rowena before she fires me," Clarissa said. "Buzz off and leave me to it."

CHAPTER TWENTY-TWO

"Maybe we've cracked the case," Sal said. He was lying on his back staring up at the sky. It wasn't fully dark yet, but it wouldn't be long. There was a sprinkling of stars out. Even though the moon was waning, it promised to be a magnificent starry night.

"That's probably what's taking her so long!" Toby sighed. "She told Ed and now they've gone to arrest the van driver and so he's gone on the run and they're chasing him down!"

"I think you have an overactive imagination," Moriarty told him. "She's probably caught in traffic."

"At this time of night?" Toby asked.

"They did say on the Twilight Barking that there

are more protests in town this evening," Sal reminded Toby.

"That's true," Toby admitted.

"Anyway, it's a great theory!" Sal patted himself on the back. Or tried to. He couldn't get his leg round and ended up twisting around and about and nearly falling over. "Meep!"

"It is!" Toby agreed, catching the rat and sitting him down. "Having said that, there are so many theories flying about, I don't know what to think."

"My personal favourite is that the biggest shop for miles around might be trying to kill off the little shops," Moriarty remarked. "Logically, you'd expect it to be the other way around."

"I'm not sure anyone killing anyone is a good look," said Toby.

"But you assassinate kings, you don't assassinate serfs," Moriarty asserted.

Moriarty could be quite bloodthirsty at times. *Goodness knows where she gets her ideas from,* Toby thought. *Maybe she reads books.* ***History*** *books. Always dangerous. She'd be better off sticking to dictionaries like me.*

"What's a serf?" Sal wanted to know.

Moriarty regarded the rat in disdain. "It's you, little pudding."

Sal balled up his fists. "I'm not anyone's dessert, crazy cat lady!"

"Main course, then." Moriarty licked her lips.

"Come on, guys," Toby intervened. "We shouldn't be fighting among ourselves."

Sal lowered his fists. Moriarty sniffed and stuck her nose in the air. Toby felt a need to rescue the situation. "To be honest, I have no clue what a serf is either."

Moriarty exhaled noisily. "A kind of peasant. Like you two. The opposite of king, if you will."

This confused Toby, who considered himself a citizen and a subject. That sounded much better than being called a peasant! He cleared his throat and valiantly tried to change the subject whilst simultaneously distracting Moriarty from the topic of killing things.

"Sal and I were saying earlier we've never been in a supermarket," he said. "Have you?"

"No." Moriarty's curiosity was evidently piqued. "I've seen them on the television, though. Do they allow animals inside, do you think?"

"Whenever I'm in the car and we pop by, Clarissa says 'no dogs allowed', but she's never mentioned no cats," Toby recalled.

"What about rats?" Sal asked.

"Nobody wants rats anywhere," Moriarty told him.

"Harsh," said Toby, *and yet undoubtedly true.*

"Hey," Sal blustered. "We get around, you know. Rats reach places cats—and dogs—can only dream of!"

"I dream of the milk aisle," Moriarty said. "Have you been there?"

"Well, no," Sal confessed. "At least not in the big shop."

"Mmm!" Toby drooled. "I dream of fish fingers."

Moriarty studied him uncertainly. "I like fish, but I didn't know they had fingers."

"The big ones do. Sharks and stuff." Toby nodded knowledgeably.

"I like milk," Sal said. "And fish. But oooh ... kweesh!"

The three animals lost themselves in thought for a moment, each dreaming of their favourite foods and looking sweetly wistful, like extras from an Oliver Twist movie. In Sal's case, 'favourite foods' amounted to a fair few.

"It would be really nice to have a look around a supermarket," Toby said. "Do some shopping." He used the term loosely. He didn't have any money so, strictly speaking, it wouldn't be 'shopping'.

Sal eyed him speculatively. "Maybe ... maybe we could. I mean ... if we checked out Sebco, that would be ... like we were looking for clues into the murders or summat, wouldn't it?"

Moriarty's eyes glinted. "That's stretching things a little too far."

Toby narrowed his eyes. "But is it though? You said yourself that erm ..."—*ooh, how to spin this?*—"serfs assassinate kings. Maybe we should go looking for serfs."

He thought Moriarty would refuse. She tended to stay close to home, stalking small beings at this end of the street or sitting on various gateposts or walls, or she'd be 'washing her hair'. But this time, she surprised them. "I would like to take a look," she said. "How far away is it?"

Toby had no real idea of the distance, but he knew it wasn't far from the park. "Not far as the crow flies," he said.

"How far does the crow fly?" Sal asked, hands on hips, stretching his spine.

Moriarty grinned. "A long way if it knows what's good for it. I do enjoy a crow supper."

"Eww," said Sal.

"Poor crow," said Toby. "Come on. Let's go."

Sal held up a tiny paw. "But how far is it? Crows

are ginormous. They can fly for miles! I've only got little legs."

"Maybe you'd better stay behind," Moriarty suggested.

Sal pouted. "Now there's no need for that. I do wanna come. I'm just mentionin' it, like, cos I don't know how far a crow flies. I mean ... does a crow fly further than a sparrow?"

"I think—" began Toby.

"Or ... or ... a great tit?"

"Sal—"

"Or what about something really huge like ..." Sal blew his furry cheeks out, trying to think of a massive bird.

"A dodo?" suggested Moriarty, deadpan.

"Guys—"

"An albatross!" roared Sal. "How does how far a crow can fly measure up to how far an albatross can fly?"

"Sal—" Toby was beginning to lose it.

Sal lifted his shoulders, his paws held out, palms up. "It makes a difference, and I wanna make sure—"

Toby wanted to cry. "It's just a stupid saying!"

"So no-one knows how far the crow flies?" Sal asked.

Moriarty inspected the claws on her left paw. "It

depends which crow we're talking about. If it's the one I caught in Mrs Crouch's garden a few weeks ago, not very far."

Sal swallowed. "Gee."

"Guys!" Toby grumbled. "Can you stop bickering for five seconds so we can get going?"

Moriarty smirked. "Of course."

Sal sniffed and moved closer to Toby, casting wary glances Moriarty's way as they set out on their journey.

Toby had a good head for navigating, while Sal had an intimate knowledge of the layout of the town. Getting to the park was easy, of course, especially in the dark with fewer people around, and then between them they found a route that took them through lots of gardens and back alleys, until eventually they could see the neon lights of the petrol station next door to Sebco.

"This is it!" Toby wagged his tail excitedly. They were hiding in a rather spiky bush on the edge of the car park but not far from the main entrance.

"It's still open." Moriarty sounded surprised.

"It's one of those twenty-four-hour places," Toby said. "Apparently Ed uses it when he's on lates."

As if on cue, a police car drove slowly past them

and pulled into a space. The creatures shrank back into the bush.

"Ow," said Toby. "Rotten prickles."

"What are the peelers doing here?" Sal asked, creeping forward. "I reckon they're onto my man. The van man! He must be here too!"

"I expect they're here to buy some supper," said Moriarty. "There's no way the van man is here."

"Oh ye of little faith," said Sal, jumping off the kerb. He darted onto the road, just as another car came towards them. Sal turned to face it, froze and shrieked, a rat in the headlights.

"Jeepers!" Toby closed his eyes, his heart in his mouth.

"Dearie dearie me," said Moriarty.

Toby dared to peek. Sal had assumed 'his' position. Lying on his back, feet in the air, eyes shut tight, tongue out.

"Hahaha!" Toby laughed nervously. "Okay, you idiot. You can get up now." When Sal didn't immediately move, Toby's knees began to quiver. It wasn't until he bounded towards the rat that Sal opened his eyes and wafted at his face.

"Phew. That was close!" he said.

"Grrrrrrr!" Toby was incandescent. "Don't do

that to me! You're shortening my life by at least a week every single time you faint!"

"A rat's gotta faint in the face of danger," said Sal. "I leave the fight and the flight to you guys."

Moriarty tutted. "Such a drama queen. Are we going in?"

"Yes, let's!" Toby stomped off, absurdly annoyed at his rotund friend. The others caught up with him a couple of yards from the doors.

"What is going on here?" Moriarty asked, watching the door appear and disappear.

"Space age," said Sal, scratching his head.

"Revolving doors," said Toby, who had sat and watched them from Clarissa's car on occasion. They sucked hoomans in and then spat some out. There always appeared to be more going in than being released for some reason. Toby had no idea what happened to the spares.

"So it *is* a door?" Sal asked, because it didn't look like anything he'd ever seen before.

"Yes," said Toby. "Watch."

The three friends stood side by side and observed a man and a woman coming out with a couple of bags each. She was clutching a bunch of flowers to her chest too.

"Awww," said Sal. "So romantic."

"Concentrate!" ordered Toby. "We need to learn how to do this."

The hoomans shuffled slowly, matching their pace to the door's turning mechanism and then, when there was enough of a gap, they moved easily through it and out into the car park.

"Seems simple enough," said Moriarty.

"What happens if we get stuck?" Sal asked.

"I guess we'll get rescued," said Toby.

"Fair enough. Let's try it!" Sal skipped forward.

Toby reached out just in time to grab his tail. "Let's do it all together, shall we?"

They waited until there were no more hoomans in sight and, even when it was all clear, they let the doors do another couple of circumnavigations until they could summon up the courage to take the leap.

"After three," said Toby. "One, two, three!" Together they sprinted between the moving door and the frame, but once inside forgot to keep walking. They paused. The doors didn't.

"Eek!" shrieked Sal, who was bringing up the rear. "I'm going to be crushed!"

"Keep moving!" Moriarty shouted, and they rushed to the front of the space, noses to the door's edge as it turned. To their right, the light became temporarily blinding and then faded away, and then dark and the car park reappeared. They kept going. Light. Faded. Dark.

"I think we need to get out at some stage," Moriarty suggested.

"What?" Sal, holding on to Toby's fur, quivered.

"Follow the light," said Moriarty. "Step out into the light!"

CHAPTER TWENTY-THREE

Once their eyes had adjusted, the lights weren't as bright as they'd initially thought, but the sensory overload had them all quaking in their boots.

Music played over some ratty old sound system. There was a fair amount of clanging coming from somewhere, and so much beeping! *Beep! Be-beep-beep!* In addition to that, the smells ... millions of them. Simply overwhelming.

"Watch out!" Moriarty warned and jumped out of the way. Instinctively, Toby grabbed Sal and followed her, just as a shopping trolley packed full of bottles of wine and beer sailed in their direction. Toby's and Moriarty's heads swung as it went past.

Toby was pleased to see that someone was pushing it and it wasn't operating of its own accord.

"Jeepers," Moriarty said. "Dangers around every corner."

Toby placed Sal on the floor and the rat promptly began drying himself off. "Ick. Dog spit."

"Could be worse, could be cat spit," said Toby.

"Mingled with rat blood," said Moriarty without looking at either of them.

Sal grunted in disgust. "Cor."

"Where are we going?" Toby asked. "We can't hide here forever." Three little heads peered out from behind the stack of pallets—tubs of chocolates by the look of them—and surveyed their surroundings. Directly ahead lay a jungle of green. Fresh scents of cabbage and broccoli, leeks and spuds, beans and carrots and ... and ... everything! And mingled with all that goodness, as if it wasn't enough, the sweeter scent of fruit.

Toby was partial to apple and carrot and the occasional roast potato, but he was far more interested in the more distant fragrance of ... hot chicken!

"Mmm," Moriarty purred. "I smell fish."

For Sal's part, he was looking disappointed. "I can't smell kweesh."

"You'll find it in the chiller," Toby replied knowledgeably. He had found it there in the minimarket, after all. "And there's one of those over there."

The three of them regarded the chiller cabinets with interest. There were three of them: one containing plastic bottles of drinks, the other two housing a variety of pre-packed products, some of which Toby recognised as sammiches. In fact, when he looked closer, he realised he'd never seen so many sammiches in one place in his entire life!

Unfortunately there was a barrier to him throwing himself into the cabinet. The two police officers they'd seen in the car park were busily selecting items. Toby glowered at them. "I don't think they're chasing our van man after all, Sal."

"Thoroughly disappointing," said Moriarty. "Now look, chaps," she said, addressing Toby. "I'm a big girl, so I want to go my own way. What say we meet back here in about ten cat minutes?"

Toby had no idea what cat minutes amounted to. "What about twenty dog minutes?" he asked, fearing that the police officers were taking a ridiculous amount of time just to choose a sammich! *Buy them all*, he thought. *Except my favourites*.

Sal looked from one to the other. "How about we just meet back when we're done?" he suggested.

"Sounds good to me," said Toby.

"Very well." Moriarty sniffed and stalked off, not in any sort of hurry, her tail in the air.

"Let's get a little closer," Toby suggested, and Sal moved up next to him and grabbed a handful of fur. "I meant to the chiller," Toby told him.

"Oh." Sal sidestepped. "Yeah. Yeah. I knew you meant that."

"I can't decide between tuna kewk or cheese and onion," the female police officer was saying.

No contest, thought Toby. *Nobody but nobody needs onion on a sammich. And what's kewk, anyway?*

"I loathe cucumber," the male officer said. "It's the devil's vegetable. But there's no way you're getting back in my car if you're eating onion!"

"It's your car now, is it?" The policewoman tittered. "What about salmon?"

"Avoid the fish. It'll stink!"

Do hurry up, thought Toby.

"That leaves me with cheese and tomato, cheese salad or ham ..."

"They sound safe. I'm having egg mayo!"

"Ugh. That's stinky too! Can I at least have cheese and onion crisps?"

"If you must." His radio crackled and a voice blurted words that made no sense. The officer listened for a second, then turned it down. "The baker protests are still going on in the marketplace," he said. "I bet we get a shout in a minute." He held up a small tub of melon and apple squares. There might have been one or two black grapes in there too, but not so you'd notice. "I'm having a pot of fruit. Look at this."

Bleugh! thought Toby.

"So healthy," the woman said. "I need to get a pint of milk too. Let's go that way."

Hooray! Toby watched as the officers walked towards the jungle aisle. Once they were a safe distance, he bounded forward and, front paws on the bottom of the fridge, gazed up at the wondrous assortment of sammiches.

Sal scurried after him. "Can you see any kweesh?" he asked.

Toby performed a quick inventory. "No kweesh," he confirmed. "Odd. I thought this was where it would be. These are sammiches, pies, pasties, fruit pots and drinks. Would you like a cheese sammich?"

"That would probably be my second choice," Sal said, looking around. "Do you think there are any more fridges?"

As if on cue, an announcement came over the tannoy, interrupting the incredibly bland music.

"Duty manager to the freezer aisle, please. Duty manager to the freezer aisle."

"Did you hear that?" Sal sat up on his back legs, twirling his tail in excitement. "A freezer aisle. A whole aisle with freezers!"

"Brrr," said Toby, distracted by a ham hock, lettuce and pickle sammich. *Do I like pickle? I'm not sure I do.*

"Thing is, if there's a freezer aisle, it stands to reason there'll be a fridge aisle too, ammiright?" Sal asked.

Toby tried to reach for the ham hock sammich with his nose. It was way out of reach. He might have to climb up. "Maybe." A thought occurred to him. "But what if the supermarket sells *actual* fridges and freezers? Think about it. They have to be sold somewhere, and it would need to be a mega shop like this one that had the room to sell them."

"True." Sal pursed his lips. "How do they get the fridges and the freezers in the shopping trolley things? Those are big, but they're not that big."

"Maybe there are bigger ones somewhere," said Toby, turning back to do an engineering survey regarding the problem of obtaining a ham hock sammich.

"You know what?" Sal asked. "I think I'll go and have a look."

"Do that," said Toby. *Now, if I climb up there and balance on one leg ...*

"Meet you back at the pallet," said Sal and zipped off.

Toby glanced around. *Thank dogness it's quiet in here,* he thought as he jumped into the chiller. *Now. One foot here and one foot there and stretchhhhhhhhhhhhh!* His nose made contact with the ham hock sammiches and he managed to knock a few down.

While I'm up here ... He wiggled to his left and headbutted the tuna mayo. *Moriarty might like one of those. What would Sal go for ... Oh!* This was easier. There were yellow stickered ham salads that had to be eaten TODAY and would no doubt taste rank. *Sal'll love them!*

Satisfied, Toby jumped out of the fridge, wondering if he should get a basket. Clarissa always used a basket. The problem was, the baskets here in Sebco were almost as big as Toby. Nope. There was nothing else for it. He'd have to levitate the sammiches.

"Up we go," he said, and three of his chosen sammiches rose into the air and hovered there. The thing was, there were several people around and he didn't want to attract attention to himself. Bad enough he was a dog in a 'dogs barred' supermarket without juggling produce around like some supernatural clown.

"But I can hide things," he muttered and made his way back to the pallets. He dropped the sammiches in the gap between them and some houseplants and stood back to survey his work. The plants needed moving around a little, but this was easily sorted. There! When he was happy, he set off with a jaunty skip, the world his oyster ... in a manner of speaking.

He followed the direction the police officers had taken through the jungle aisle. This was quite amazing to Toby. He'd never seen such mountains of fresh produce. Every now and then he would stop to have a sniff or to peer under the shelves and cabinets at the wonderful array of dropped goodies. They were mainly borlie-shaped things that liked to roll: tomatoes, onions and apples, for example, but there were some other weird things too. An ugly swede, a bright-green cauliflower and some odd-shaped white and green things that looked like a cross between squashed onions and carrot tops.

He decided against snaffling these things.

Holy macaroni! At the very top of the jungle

aisle was the cheese counter! A shrink-wrapped paradise for cheese-loving dogs and rats! Toby had never seen so much cheese in his life. White cheese, yellow cheese, orange cheese, cheese with mould, cheese with bits in, soft cheese, hard cheese, cheese with red rind, cheese with holes in—*what in the cheating dairymaid is that all about?*—cheese in big triangles wrapped in fancy wrapping and smooshed inside a little wooden carton, cheese in small triangles, wrapped in foil and smooshed into a cardboard carton.

Has Sal seen this? Toby hadn't noticed which way the rat had gone. *Shall I take some with me? Or shall I ... hmmm.* Toby concentrated and lifted a sizable piece of cheddar—you can't beat cheddar—and a banana-shaped piece of cheese with a red rind and levitated them downwards till they were about a foot off the ground. Then rather than march them back over to where he'd stored his sammiches, he imagined them there, hidden among the plants, before mentally pushing the items away in that direction. It was effortless. The cheeses mooched through the air happily enough and disappeared out of sight.

"This is a brilliant way of doing the shopping!" said Toby. "I should patent this. Or at the very least teach Clarissa how to do it!"

Satisfied, Toby skipped around the corner and gazed in wonder at the sight that met him. All along the back wall of the store were smaller counters. Closest to him, fish. Far away, the bakery. In between, meat.

And aisles and aisles of goodies!

He made his way past the fish counter. Presumably Moriarty had found this, but he couldn't see her. Not immediately anyway. It was only when he walked past and scanned left and right that he spotted her through a set of double doors marked 'Staff Only', where she was crouching over an enormous fish, still with most of its skin, chomping away on its belly.

Jeez, Moriarty. You won't need to eat for a month if you get through all that.

He left her to it though, opting instead to go in search of Sal and see how he was faring with his kweesh quest. Along the way he passed a stationery section on the end of the aisle, and he paused there gazing at all the colourful objects. Toby loved to draw—even though he wasn't very good at it—and his colouring pencils were becoming worn, having been sharpened down to stubs. *Would it be terribly wrong to ...*

Oops! He managed to dislodge a pack of forty-eight colouring pencils and send them floating off to his plant hideout.

Cool!

The next aisle contained biscuits, all of them packaged in bright wrappers. *Mmm, biscuits.* Toby sauntered down, heading towards the tills at the front of the shop, searching for the digestives, his favourite favourite.

But his happy reverie was rudely interrupted by a shrill scream.

He stopped, eyes swivelling, ears tweaking.

The scream came again.

And a woman shouting something unintelligible.

Toby cowered against the shelves as several members of staff shot past the end of his aisle. *Uh-oh.*

When the woman shouted again, this time he heard the word 'rat'!

Rumbled.

He sensed movement from behind and spun around, expecting trouble. It was Moriarty, running faster than he'd ever seen her. "Time to get out of here," she said, skidding to a halt beside him. "I'm full anyway."

"We can't go anywhere without Sal," Toby told her.

"Are you kidding me? Wherever he is—"

"The kweesh aisle—"

"There are going to be lots of hoomans! They don't like rats in their food. You know that!"

"Sure, but I can't leave—"

"Pssst!"

Toby and Moriarty froze.

"Psssst!"

Their heads swivelled.

"Up. Here!"

Toby tipped his head back and there, way up on the very top of the shelving where the biscuits were stored in brown boxes, a teeny bewhiskered face stared down at them.

"What are you doing up there?" Toby hissed.

"I had to make a quick getaway," said Sal. "I left all me delectables behind. My life was in great danger!"

"We need to leave," Moriarty told him. "Now!"

"No kidding," said Sal.

Toby took a step back so he could see Sal better. "Come down."

"I thought I'd jump from shelf to shelf," said Sal, standing on his hind legs and looking around. "It should be safe with all the hoomans busy in the cold aisle!"

Toby calculated the distance between shelves.

Seven or eight feet? How far can rats jump? "Come down, Sal!" he insisted.

"And hurry!" Moriarty was beginning to get annoyed. "Or I'll come up there and get you myself."

"It might come to that," said Toby.

"I won't bring him down in one piece though, fuzzball features! Is that what you want?"

"Ah." Toby nodded. "Hurry up, Sal!" he called.

"A'right, a'right. Keep your fur on!" Sal squinted down and slithered to the edge of the shelf. He needed footholds—which was a little difficult because the shelf underneath was half empty, leaving him nothing to grasp. He swung himself over the edge, his front paws holding on to the top shelf for dear life, then tried to swing his rotund body backwards and forwards so he could land on the shelf below.

He let go at the wrong moment, swinging outwards rather than inwards.

Toby and Moriarty stared up in disbelief.

"How can one rat get everything so wrong?" asked Toby.

"Terminal velocity," remarked Moriarty, with an edge of glee that Toby didn't appreciate.

Sal arced through the air, his little legs scrabbling around, seeking to gain purchase where there was none. Toby, eyes on the prize, shifted his weight this way and that, judging the right moment to open his mouth and try to catch poor Sal, while simultaneously fearing he'd miss.

Before he could begin his leap, a black shadow catapulted upwards and snatched the rat out of the air. Sal shrieked and fainted—of course—and Moriarty landed nimbly on the floor beside Toby, all four paws hitting the ground silently.

Before Toby could catch his breath and beg her not to eat the rat, she unceremoniously dropped her prey at his paws. "I told you I was full," she said.

"I think I need CPR," Toby gasped. "My heart has stopped."

"So's his!" Moriarty indicated the pale rat.

"He'll be alright," Toby said, nudging Sal.

Sal opened one eye. "Am I dead?"

"Moriarty saved your life!" said Toby.

Moriarty snickered. "And now you'll forever be indebted to me."

"Thank you," said Sal. "I think."

"Can we go now?" asked Moriarty. "I've done my good deed for the day."

"Can you walk?" Toby asked Sal. "Or do I need to give you a lift?"

"A lift sounds good," Sal said weakly, laying it on a little thick as he rubbed cat spit off his fur.

"Climb on then," said Toby. "I found some sammiches earlier, so we'll collect those on our way out." He crouched down so that Sal could jump aboard.

"I couldn't eat another thing," Moriarty said, but she licked her lips anyway. "Come on, let's go while all the hoomans are busy looking for Sal in the wrong aisle."

They made their way down the biscuit aisle to the bottom facing the bank of self-checkouts, fortunately completely deserted. From there they turned right and headed for the revolving doors. The jungle aisle, the potted plants and the pallets of chocolate tubs were close enough to touch when Toby suddenly stopped dead.

"What's up?" Moriarty asked. "Come on. Let's grab our things and go!"

"Him!" Toby gestured at a man near the sammich chiller.

"He's choosing a sandwich. So what?" Moriarty pushed against Toby, trying to force him closer to the exit.

Toby took a few steps, but not towards the

revolving doors, more towards the chiller. He skirted past the plants so he could see more clearly.

"Uh-oh," said Sal.

The man, wearing a fluorescent vest and a baseball cap, wasn't selecting a sammich—he was fiddling with the paper cups stacked beside the coffee machine. He had a small plastic bag in one hand containing some sort of powder, and he was sprinkling it on and around the cups.

Toby's jaw dropped open.

The man turned.

Sal squealed. "Van Man!"

CHAPTER TWENTY-FOUR

The man regarded Toby in surprise as Toby gaped back at him.

"Dogs aren't allowed in here," he said and walked past Toby without otherwise batting an eyelid. Toby, still slack-jawed, turned to watch him go, imagining he would walk out of the shop without a backward glance. Instead, Van Man picked up a basket from the pile by the door and made a beeline for the jungle aisle.

"What are we going to do?" Sal whispered. "That must be poison."

"Must it?" Moriarty asked, sounding more doubtful.

"Oh, hey," exclaimed Sal. "Why don't you go

and lick up some of that powder and see what happens to you?"

"I'm only saying maybe he wanted a coffee and that was that awful fake sugar stuff," Moriarty said. "We shouldn't jump to conclusions."

"It was definitely Van Man," Toby replied, his tone grim. "You didn't see the photos."

"That's true."

"We need to tell Clarissa so she can let Ed know," said Toby, wishing he had a mobile phone or something. Unfortunately, canine mobile phones were yet to be invented—and besides, he had nowhere to store one.

"But that means leaving the supermarket," Sal said. "Anyone could come in and try and buy a drink."

"We need to create a mess," said Toby. "Hoomans don't like messes." He had a sudden idea. "Sal! Get up there and dislodge the cups!" He stood on his hind legs and Sal manoeuvred over his shoulder blades, across his snout and up onto the counter.

"Whatever you do, don't inhale that powder," warned Moriarty. "If it is what you think it is, that would spell the end for you!"

Spell ... Toby watched Sal scurrying towards the

paper cups. What if the customers—or the staff—simply collected together the cups and restacked them? It wouldn't be enough. *More mess,* he thought. *We need to make a lot more mess.*

The coffee machine itself seemed like a complicated item. It had a computer screen and a couple of buttons.

The first stack of cups toppled over. Given how light they were, they didn't make much noise as they hit the floor. Lots of them remained tucked inside each other.

"Moriarty," Toby said. "Get shredding!"

Moriarty grasped the idea immediately and pounced on the cups, murderously unsheathing her sharp claws. Within seconds, half a dozen cups lay in tatters. *Pawesome!*

Sal sent another stack of cups down, and then a third. Two more to go. Toby turned back to the machine. He couldn't read it from this angle, but he understood that there must be lists of drinks you could order.

Out of the corner of his eye, movement momentarily grabbed his attention. He turned. Van Man, clutching a banana and a pint of milk, stood next to the pallets, watching the animals' antics.

"Get away from there!" Van Man hissed. "Should I call security?"

Toby considered this rich given that here was a man intent on poisoning half of Sun Valley, *and* he hadn't paid for his shopping *either*, by the looks of it.

"I don't have time for you," said Toby and redirected his attention to the coffee machine. "*Pour*," he said, imagining pushing the buttons one by one. "Flow freely like a river!"

The coffee machine began to drip.

"Get away from there!" Van Man was angry now, his voice louder.

"*Pour*!" Toby told the machine. "Free and fast!"

Coffee spurted. Sal knocked the final stack of cups down to Moriarty, who was snarling in a way Toby had never heard a cat do before.

Van Man rushed forward. "Get away!" he bellowed, knocking Toby sideways and sending him crashing into a display of cauliflowers before making a grab for Sal, who nimbly jumped into the sammich chiller and scurried out of Van Man's reach.

Toby yelped but struggled back to his feet. Raising his voice to a high-pitched wail, he roared, "*Unleash the dam*!" and sent his energy forward like a bouncing bomb.

The coffee machine gurgled and spat.

Van Man reached for Moriarty and grabbed her by the scruff of her neck. She yowled and twisted in his grip, raking his hands with her needle-like claws. Van Man shrieked and let go, tucking his hands beneath his armpits.

"What's going on over here?" a man's voice yelled. Toby hunkered down beside the cauliflowers as a man in a Sebco uniform approached. "Can I get some security to the front of the shop, please?" he shouted. "Security?"

A thunder of boots from the far side of the shop, where no doubt plenty of workers were still searching for a rat in the fridges.

"*Pour*!" sang Toby, and finally the coffee machine gave in. With a loud belch, coffee exploded out in all directions, spattering the sammich chillers and walls, pouring over the sides of the counter, onto the floor and covering the piles of shredded card Moriarty had worked hard to produce.

People in uniform were descending on them from all corners. Van Man made a dive for the revolving doors and disappeared through them.

"Outta here!" yelled Sal and went in after him.

Moriarty and Toby dashed towards the doors just as Sal's section closed. They waited a few—heart-in-mouth—moments until a new gap opened up, then threw themselves inside and began pushing with all their might against the glass partition.

"Was that a dog?" someone was asking.

"Have you seen the mess? What's happened here?"

"Someone call the police."

"Can't this thing go any faster?" asked Moriarty.

Toby gazed up, wondering if he could conjure a spell that would cause the revolving doors to spin a little faster, but the rush of fresh air in their faces told them they were almost outside. And besides, who knew what would have happened if the spell had gone wrong.

They leapt out into the car park to be greeted by an overexcited Sal. "This way! This way!" he was shouting, gesturing to his left.

"What's this way?" Toby asked.

"Van Man! He's getting away!" Sal screeched off, leaving Toby and Moriarty in his dust.

They exchanged looks. "He has a van," Moriarty reminded Toby. "We can't chase a van."

Toby peered in the direction Sal had taken. "Sal is."

"He's crazy."

"That's true, but I can't let him go alone."

"And to think I could have been at home

washing my ears in front of the fire," Moriarty grumbled. "Very well. Lead the way."

Toby hurried after Sal, eyes and ears straining to catch sight or sound of his friend. In a badly lit car park, on a dark evening, it wasn't easy to see anything, let alone something as small as a rat.

Instead, they spotted the van first. The cream and coffee colour of the paintwork stood out despite the muted light. The logo was instantly recognisable too, the cheery coffee cup an anti-metaphor for what they'd left behind them inside the supermarket.

"Hurry," urged Toby as the van's lights blinked on.

"Where's the rat?" Moriarty asked.

"I have no idea," Toby answered. "He wouldn't have climbed in, would he?"

Toby edged around the van to the passenger side and stared up at the window. There, peering down at them for the second time tonight, was Sal's sweet little face.

"Eeek! Get out of there, you ... you idiot!" Toby's two front paws performed a tap dance.

Sal stuck his tongue out.

The van made a noise rather like Clarissa's car did whenever she tried to put it in reverse. Toby rapidly made up his mind. He was getting Sal out of that van one way or another.

"I wonder what's in the back," he said to Moriarty. "I need to draw Van Man to the rear."

"More cups, probably," Moriarty said. "We already know they don't make a great deal of noise, so they're useless as a distraction." Moriarty's eyes elongated. "We could give him a flat tyre?"

"How are we going to do that?"

Moriarty unleashed one claw. It sparkled as it caught the light of the massive neon Sebco sign on the supermarket roof. Funnily enough, to Toby it didn't remotely resemble a cat claw, more a minuscule sword or dagger or something similar ... with an extremely sharp blade.

She didn't wait for Toby to respond, simply stalked around the van to the offside rear tyre with Toby on her heels. Moriarty wasn't messing. She stabbed deep into the rubber tyre three or four times in quick succession. "*Campestris*!" she spat.

The tyre hissed and began to bulge.

"Crikey," said Toby, impressed. "Did you just do *magick*?"

"Mind your own business," said Moriarty and marched him back around to the passenger side.

Van Man must have realised he had trouble

almost instantaneously, because he turned the engine off and jumped out of his cab. That was the cue for Toby to open the passenger door. He waved a paw. "*Open*!" he ordered, and the enormous van door swung wide, Sal riding the handle like a surfer rides a wave.

"Come on out!" urged Toby.

"No!" Sal shouted back, folding his arms and scowling down at them. "We can't let him get away with poisoning people!"

"We can't do anything about it right at this minute! We need a hooman—"

"There's no time!" Sal yelled.

"I fear he's right," Moriarty said.

"We have to find a way!" Sal insisted. "We should go with him now. See if we can force him to hand himself in to the police."

"How are we going to do that?" Toby argued. "Better we go and find Clarissa and tell her what's gone on. She can tell Ed and they can track—"

"He's coming back," whispered Moriarty. "Get in the van."

"I don't want to get in the van!" Toby shouted. "I don't want to be dognapped!"

"It's not dognapping if you go voluntarily," Moriarty told him.

"Are you sure?"

"Get in the van!" Moriarty poked Toby hard. He hoped she hadn't used her supersharp magickal claw or he'd bleed to death before anyone noticed, but he finally took the hint and—with great difficulty—clambered into the cab and onto the passenger seat, almost squishing a banana that had been left there. He pushed it off the seat and sat down.

Moriarty leapt gracefully up onto the seat beside him in two elegant bounds. "Shut the door," she said, and Toby imagined closing it. It swung shut, catapulting Sal against the pair of them so that they tumbled together into a kind of scraggly furry heap with lots of eyes and tails and teeth.

Van Man plopped into the driver's seat and stared down at them in a combination of surprise, irritation and horror.

"Hello," said Toby, from beneath Sal's cushiony bottom.

"What the blazes? Are you the same pests from inside?"

"Maybe," said Toby.

"Definitely," said Sal, straightening his tail out. It had become a little kinked and he was worried Toby would mistake it for spaghetti.

"You don't want to mess with us," said Moriarty, obviously deciding the other two were being too nice.

"No, you don't," Toby agreed. "I left my sammiches behind and that makes me really angry."

"Hangry," said Sal.

"And you won't like him when he's hangry," said Moriarty. "I mean, it's hard to like him when he's not hangry, to be honest."

"Not that there are many times when our Tobes 'ere ain't hungry," Sal said.

"Do you mind?" Toby asked. "Casting misper— disper— asper—"—*dang, what was the word*—"slandering me! Besides, you two can talk!"

"Get out of here!" Van Man spat and leaned over to open the door, with the probable intention of shoving them out, thought Toby. "I don't need all that noise!"

But Moriarty unleashed her claws once more and the man jerked his arm away. "Jeezus! You wanna go for a drive, do you?"

"Not really," said Toby.

"We're going wherever you go," declared Moriarty.

Van Man sneered. "You'll live to regret it!"

"Let's hope you do too," said Toby. "Buckle up, kids, we're going on a joyride!"

CHAPTER TWENTY-FIVE

The van lurched backwards as Van Man threw it into reverse.

Sal, who had only now righted himself properly, was catapulted forward. He face-planted against the dashboard and fell into the footwell.

"You okay?" Toby leaned over to check, imagining Sal would be lying toes up with his tongue out—as per usual—but instead saw him wrestling with the banana.

"I'm fine," said Sal. "Don't worry about me."

"Fair enough," said Toby and retreated to the back of the seat.

The van made a series of peculiar noises as it rolled backwards, lurching a little and feeling oddly out of balance.

"I think the back tyre is still flat," said Moriarty. "He couldn't fix it. I made sure of that."

Toby regarded her doubtfully. "Should he still be driving, do we think?"

"Obviously not, but let him make a rod for his own back," she purred.

"What if we crash? It's the rod I'll need for my own back that's worrying me!"

Van Man swung the wheel and straightened up but then jammed on the brakes and swore like a sailor.

"Well, really," said Moriarty, tipping forward.

Toby peered out of the front window. Blue lights were flashing at the entrance to the supermarket's car park as a patrol car—maybe even the one they'd seen earlier—trundled slowly along. "Police," he said, excited at the prospect of being rescued so soon.

"Shut up, dog!" Van Man threw his hand out to knock Toby from his perch. Toby growled at him, peeling his lips back and showing his teeth. "Flamin' Nora!" Van Man slapped his hand against the steering wheel then leaned over, studying the police car's movements, and began biting his fingernails.

The car stopped directly in front of the revolving doors—which were no longer revolving—and two officers jumped out and rushed inside.

Van Man exhaled noisily. "Right," he muttered. "Come on."

He allowed the van to roll forwards, his head swivelling this way and that. The rear tyre made a squelching sound. The faster he drove, the more repetitive the sound. He took it steadily until he reached the car park's exit, before indicating and moving out onto the main road. There wasn't much traffic around so he made quick progress.

Sal suddenly appeared at the edge of the passenger seat carrying the banana. "Help me," he demanded, and so Toby dutifully leaned forward once more and yanked him up beside them.

"Get off that!" Van Man reached out and snatched the banana. "That's my supper!"

"You didn't pay for it," Toby challenged him. Van Man couldn't understand what he was saying, but that didn't mean Toby was going to remain quiet for long. "Do you really want to share your banana with a rat?" he asked.

"Shut up, guv'nor," Sal said. "I don't got germs!"

"Of course you do," said Toby. "Didn't rats carry the Black Death?"

"I think you'll find that it was fleas wot decimated half the world with the plague," said Sal. "I'm not taking the rap for no fleas. I ain't got fleas."

"The amount of barfs you take, that's not surprising."

"I like barfs," said Sal. "I likes smellin' nice!"

"Can you all just pipe down?" Van Man demanded. "I'm trying to think here!"

"Thinking is hard work," said Sal. "Eat yer banana."

Toby peered down at Sal quizzically. Sal performed jazz hands. "I could do with a barf right now," he said and winked.

"What should I do? What should I do?" Van Man mumbled, tapping his fingers to a rhythm only he could hear. The van was not driving well, forcing Van Man to take it slowly. He'd already been flashed and beeped at by a couple of drivers.

"Drive to the police station," Moriarty suggested, her gaze boring into the side of Van Man's head. "Let's finish this now."

The cab suddenly lit up like a disco—or rather a disco if the only flashing lights were blue—and Van Man whimpered. For a moment Toby thought he would put his foot down and take off, trying to outrun a police car with a heavy van on only three tyres. Instead, he flicked his indicators and moved into the bus stop space. There was a loud blast of a siren and a fire engine steamed past them.

"Hahahahahaha," Van Man laughed, chewing on his thumbnail. There wasn't much left of it.

Toby stared at the world outside. The park was to his left. They were heading out of Sun Valley towards Exeter. There would be more traffic when they eventually hit the main road.

"They'll have cameras, won't they?" Van Man asked.

Toby, Moriarty and Sal stared up at him. Was he talking to them? He stared out of the front window, pinching his lips together.

"There'll be cameras in the supermarket. If it wasn't for you guys, I'd have made it in and out of there without any fuss. But now, they're going to be looking for me—or someone who looks like me, with a baseball cap ..." He wound down his window, grabbed the baseball cap from his head and threw it outside across to the next lane. Its absence could be discerned by the line of compressed hair around his scalp.

"They'll be circulating my description." He peeled the banana and broke half of the fruit off, stuffing it into his mouth all at once.

The animals watched him. He must have felt them staring because he turned to them once more. "What? You hungry?" He made the banana dance a

Hawaiian hula, the little yellow skirt swirling merrily.

"No," said Sal.

"Aren't you?" Toby asked him. "That's a novelty."

"Definitely not," said Sal, "and neither are you!"

"You hungry, kitten?" Van Man asked.

"Ick," said Moriarty. "Not for banana."

"You're all too fussy," said Van Man, stuffing the second half of the banana in his mouth before throwing the hula skirt out onto the road.

"I hate litterbugs," said Toby.

"If it weren't for litterbugs I'd have starved a long time ago," said Sal, still gazing up at Van Man, his beady black eyes expectant.

"Ooh," said Van Man. He wafted at his face. A fine sheen of perspiration had begun to bead on his forehead. "Oof."

"What's up with him?" Moriarty asked.

Van Man swiped at his face. "Better get going," he said and shifted the gears. The van lurched forward and out onto the road. Toby could see sweat shining above Van Man's upper lip. Van Man blinked and changed up, forcing the van to go faster. They were approaching the outskirts of town now, where the country lanes began and where there were steep inclines, cliff edges, the bendiest of tight curves and endless forest. Eventually they would reach a roundabout and a dual carriageway, where they would mingle with other traffic on its way to Exeter or the motorway.

"We can't make it on three tyres, can we?" Moriarty asked, digging her claws deep into the fabric of the seat.

"I shouldn't have thought so," said Toby, valiantly gripping with his own claws. Only Sal appeared to be enjoying himself, one tiny fist pumping the air as he glared at Van Man, the other wrapped around Toby's front leg.

"Awww!" Van Man shifted in his seat, rocking from butt cheek to butt cheek. "Ow."

Toby stared down at Sal. "What's going on?" he asked.

"Arrrrrgh!" Van Man leaned forward. "Arrr."

"A taste of his own medicine," said Sal.

Van Man choked and threw on the brakes. By some miracle, the animals kept their seat. Van Man leaned sideways and threw up out of the window.

"Ewwwwww!" the three onlookers chorused.

"Oh, that's grim," said Moriarty, as though she'd never coughed up a hairball in her entire life.

"Ugh. Ugh. Ohhh. Ow," Van Man moaned, flapping at his face, the sweat pouring off him.

Toby surveyed Van Man warily before turning to Sal again. "What do you mean by a taste of his own medicine?"

Sal held up his paws. "I'm covered in that powder he was waving around on the cups in the supermarket. I rubbed myself all over the banana—"

"You what?" Toby could hardly believe his furry ears. "The poison will have transferred to the banana. He'll have had that all over his hands. That ... that's murder, Sal!"

"I doubt there was enough to kill him," said Sal. The van lurched forward. "Was there?"

Van Man had gone awfully quiet. Toby turned that way to see him slumping in his seat. "Who knows how much it takes? He doesn't look ... well."

"Oh dear," said Sal.

"Let's get out," said Moriarty. But before they could magick open the door, Van Man's foot slipped off the brake.

"He put the handbrake on, didn't he?" asked Toby, ducking his head trying to see. The problem being, in a van, the handbrake is on the side nearest the door, not in the middle where you'd find the handbrake in a car.

The van was sliding forwards.

"Oh no," said Toby.

"Erm ... open the door ..." Moriarty said.

The van began to pick up speed. Three pairs of eyes stared out of the windscreen at the road ahead. They couldn't see much except the white and black chevrons that indicated a tight bend.

"Oh my life," said Sal.

"Oh *your* life?" Toby asked. "What about *my* life? What about Moriarty's life?"

"Do something, Toby!" Moriarty cried.

"What do you think I can do? Drive?" The moment he said the word, he knew exactly what he needed to do. He jumped into the driver's seat on top of the unconscious Van Man and quickly made a study of the dashboard. The gears were high up but virtually the same as Clarissa's car. The steering wheel ... was a steering wheel. He placed his front paws on it as they drove towards the curve ... and turned it.

The tyres squealed. He'd spun a little too sharply. "Easy, boy," he told himself. "Gently, gently ..." This time when he edged the steering wheel around, the van navigated the bend easily. Toby breathed with relief.

"We should turn around," Moriarty said. "Go back to town."

"Where would you suggest I do that?" Toby asked. "I can't do a three-point turn in this thing on a road this narrow. If I try, we'll end up going off the road."

"Oh my life," said Sal again. "I'm sorry ..."

"You will be if you kill me," said Moriarty. "I'll haunt you in a million different ways!"

"We'll just have to go forwards until I can turn around," said Toby, concentrating on the road ahead and making his paws work the wheel. *A gentle tug down here and around to the left ... Oooh, ooh ... back to the right .... Wheeee!*

With the window still down, the breeze riffled through Toby's hair. He glanced out and realised he could see behind in the wing mirror. "Hey, cool!" he said.

"Watch out, Toby!" Moriarty cried.

Toby looked forward and yanked on the steering wheel. Somehow he'd drifted into the right-hand lane and oncoming traffic. His bowels turned to ice. *Concentrate*, he thought, but risked another glance at the lights behind him. There seemed to be a fair few.

He kept going, his eyes strained, his legs tired. The

van's engine sounded loud and cross, but he didn't want to try to change gear. In addition, the juddering was getting worse, and Toby decided this was probably because of the rear tyre. It seemed a long, long time until, finally, they approached the roundabout. Toby knew it was a roundabout because multiple signs told him so.

The roundabout presented new problems.

"Guys," he said. "How do I brake?"

"Brake?" Moriarty asked. The only times she'd travelled in a vehicle before today, she'd been safely installed in her travel basket.

"Clarissa uses her feet," said Toby, "but I can't reach."

"Oh my life," said Sal.

"I swear if you say that one more time, I'm going to snuff your little life out," spat Moriarty.

"That's not helping," warned Toby. "I'm coming right up on this roundabout now and there'll be loads of traffic—"

There were streetlights here, illuminating the road, and Toby gazed left and right. "Which way round do we go?"

"Follow everyone else," Moriarty suggested.

"There isn't anyone," Toby said.

"You just said there'd be loads of traffic—"

Toby grimaced. "I think they're all behind me. I'm not sure I'm driving fast enough."

"Presumably you can do what you want then," Moriarty asserted. "I mean, isn't that what right of way means?"

"Does it?" Toby decided to take her word for it and, as he came to the junction, swung the steering wheel hard to the right so that he turned 180 degrees and back onto the lane that would take them into Sun Valley.

The instant he did that, vehicles descended on him, travelling at speed, from all directions. Horns blared, lights flashed. "Meeeeep!" Toby squealed and closed his eyes.

"Don't close your eyes!" Moriarty screeched. "You need to see where you're going!"

"Oh, yeah!" Wincing, Toby opened his eyes and straightened the steering wheel. Behind them a car honked away like a rabid goose.

"Alright, fella!" Toby leaned out of the window and flipped the bird. This only enraged the driver even further, and the honking became more frantic.

"The art of living dangerously," sighed Moriarty. "Just get us home, Toby."

"Listen, he's lucky I don't turn him into a zebra crossing," said Toby, who didn't know any spells that would turn people into any type of crossing—zebra, pelican or otherwise.

"We're still going to have the issue of how we come to a stop," said Sal. "What if I stamped on the brake pedal?"

"You wouldn't be heavy enough," Toby said.

"Maybe I could do it." Moriarty craned forward to peer into the footwell. This wasn't easy because a large portion of Van Man's body was slumped in there.

"Maybe," said Toby.

"Which one is the brake?" Moriarty asked, sliding off her seat and between Van Man's legs.

"Erm ..." Toby had no idea.

"Is that all you do?" Sal asked. "You just stamp on the brake and the van stops?"

"I guess so." Toby was concentrating on the bends, but was it his imagination or could he see lights up ahead? Were they nearly back in Sun Valley? He crossed his toes and then decided he needed his front toes to concentrate on manoeuvring the steering wheel, so he uncrossed them.

"What do the other pedals do?" Moriarty asked.

"Well ... erm ... one makes the van go faster ..."

"For the love of dogs, do NOT step on that one," Sal implored.

"And I think the other one is the clutch because Clarissa is always moaning about the clutch and Ed says she 'rides' it. Whatever that means—" Toby smiled out of the window. "The park! We're back in Sun Valley!"

"Shall I try one of these pedals now?" Moriarty called up.

"No!" Sal said, jumping onto the driver's seat with Toby and poking him. "Do you know what we should do, guv'nor?"

"Go on," said Toby, but warily, because there were more cars around now, plus some of the ones behind him were overtaking and beeping and glaring at him and shouting really rude things and using bad words. A dog can become paranoid, you know?

"Let's drop him off at the police station!" Sal said, tugging at Toby's fur. "We'll look like heroes!"

Toby liked this idea. "Yeah! There might even be a reward like in the cowboy films."

"Cor!" said Sal. "Wanted Dead or Alive: Reward five thousand kweeshes."

"Yeah! Let's do it!" Toby swung hard on the steering wheel, forcing the van around a left-hand corner. There was a poof sound and a clang and the rear of the van dropped. "I think that was the last of the tyre," Toby said, glancing in the mirror. Sparks flew. "Oooh." He decided not to share that news with Sal and Moriarty.

One right turn and then a left and another right, and the police station—complete with scaffolding—hove into view.

"We're almost there, Moriarty!" Toby called.

"Have we decided which pedal to go for?" Moriarty asked. "Left, middle or right?"

A pair of figures were standing together beside a car. "Is that Ed?" Toby asked, leaning over the steering wheel to see better. "Yes, it is. And he has Clarissa with him." As he said this, the couple turned to regard the approaching van. A look of horror crossed Clarissa's face. Ed did a double take.

"Left, middle or right?" Moriarty bellowed.

"Erm ..." Toby, in the absence of absolute knowledge, did a mental ippy-dippy-dation. *Decisions, decisions*, he thought.

"LEFT, MID—"

"Right!" Toby yelled as the van mounted the pavement and careered towards the parked car. "RIGHT!"

The van jumped forward.

Crunch.

There was a smashing of glass and a chewing up of metal, and a shocking jolt forwards that threw

Toby up on the dashboard, and backwards so that he landed on Van Man's chest. *Ooof*. He tasted blood. *Oh no, I'm dying*, he thought. Moriarty yowled. Steam hissed, escaping in a cloud from the crumpled bonnet.

Then someone flung his door open and Toby found himself staring into the face of a wide-eyed Clarissa and a ghostly pale Ed.

"What the knickerbocker glory is going on?" Ed asked.

"Toby?" Clarissa reached inside for him. "Are you hurt?"

"That was my car!" Ed shouted.

"Oops," said Toby, and wagged his tail.

Just a little.

EPILOGUE

Clarissa slipped her phone into her pocket. "That was Ed. They've charged Mark Sisker with the murders of Mayor Casterford, Cathy Burns and Jake Pike and the attempted murder of unknown others at Sebco's and Groggs."

"Mark Sisker being Van Man?" Toby asked.

"Yep." Clarissa smiled down at him. They were walking towards the marketplace having just visited the library, where Toby—much to his consternation—had been forced to wait outside. The absolute cheek of it! "They know I read, do they?" he'd asked, and Clarissa had hushed him.

"It's taken them a while to charge him," Toby complained. "It was an open-and-shut case to my mind."

Clarissa chuckled. "Well, given Sal nearly killed him with the poison he repurposed—"

"That was Van Man's fault. Don't do the crime if you can't do the time," Toby sang.

"I get that. I'm just saying he was in the hospital for four days!"

"Couldn't have happened to a nicer man," Toby muttered, failing to feel a modicum of sympathy for the murderer. "So why did he do it? Did he confess?"

"Apparently he's a coeliac."

"A what-ee-ac?"

"A coeliac. Do you remember Cathy talking about people who can't eat wheat?"

"Erm, yes." *Vaguely.*

Clarissa nodded. "Sisker has suffered symptoms for years and was recently diagnosed. Seems he's a tad bitter about it."

Toby couldn't believe his furry ears. "So, he decided to kill people because he can't eat bread?"

"It kind of makes sense in a warped way," Clarissa said doubtfully. "At least to him."

"How did he do it?" Toby skipped along beside Clarissa. "I need deets."

"Deets?"

"Details. I'm down with the kids."

"Mmm." Clarissa rolled her eyes. "I'm going to

be writing this up later. Are you sure you wouldn't rather wait until you get to read it before I send it off to Rowena?"

"No, I need to know now," said Toby. "What happens if a delivery van runs me off the road and I never find out? Squishes me? They're hard to control, those vans. Take it from me."

"Hmmm. Please don't try and drive again, Toby—"

"I'm an amazing driver," Toby said. "If Moriarty hadn't hit the wrong pedal, Ed's car would have lived to drive another day. But anyway, tell me how Van Man did it!"

"He gained easy access to the bakeries because he delivered to all of them. He didn't have to break in. The bakers knew him and let him drop his boxes in without batting an eyelid. It seems for the bakers, he scattered poison in actual ceramic mugs. First in The Magick Muffin. Remember we saw Mayor Casterford drinking tea from Dee Dee's mug?"

"I don't remember that," Toby said. "I've had a bump on the head since then."

"Poor Floof." Clarissa stopped and crouched down beside him to gently massage his head. "Better?"

"A bit," Toby said, sounding pitiful even to him. "Go on."

"The same at Cathy's. The poison was in the mug. It was her favourite mug, and she used it both in the shop and the flat. Sisker laced it when he popped out the back."

"And Groggs?"

"Sounds like that was random. Sisker didn't have a specific target. He dropped the cups off intending to harm customers, but Jake Pike must have handled them. He drew the shortest straw. The customers were luckier."

"We saw Sisker delivering to Scrumpy Dumpy's—"

"I know. But no trace of poison has been found there."

"*You* drank out of a mug while you were there!"

Clarissa nodded. "A lucky escape, I think."

Toby shivered. "And then he went after Sebco's."

Clarissa scruggled his ears. "Thank goodness you guys intervened. That could have resulted in any number of victims."

"Do you think Ed will ever forgive me?" Toby asked mournfully. So far the detective had been more than a little grumpy with the errant hound.

"Of course he will!" Clarissa sounded confident. "When he's had some sleep—"

"Not long then." This thought cheered Toby up no end.

"And the insurance company has paid out for his car."

Toby's not insubstantial eyebrows knitted together. "How long will that be?"

"How long's a piece of string?" Clarissa asked, which was not the answer Toby was after. "Come on."

They resumed their stroll. The marketplace was busy, as it usually was at lunchtime. They paused outside Cathy's Cakes. The shop was covered in scaffolding, getting a new front window and door. Inside, the shelves had been removed and painters were hard at work. As Clarissa stared at the floor above, a familiar figure stepped out of the gap where the door should be and greeted her.

"Bryn!" she said. "Good to see you!"

"You too," Bryn said, leaning down to fuss Toby.

"Are you doing it up to sell?" Clarissa asked, indicating the workers.

"Oh, no! Big change for me." He beamed. "I'm taking it on!"

"Are you closing Bryn's Bakes?"

"Not at all. I shall run both businesses side by side. I couldn't close this shop. It's where it all started, after all. I'm going to keep this as the bakery it's always been, focusing on great local bakes and cheaper eats."

"You're saving Sun Valley's Devon Split?" Clarissa asked.

"Absolutely!" Bryn laughed. "I inherited the secret of the county's best Devon Split from my mother too, you know."

"I'm so pleased," said Clarissa and hugged him. "I'll be popping in to buy one as soon as you reopen."

"Make that two," said Toby.

"On the house," said Bryn and waved her away.

"Such good news," Clarissa said to Toby as they navigated around the marketplace. "I'll write all this up later. It's going to make for an amazing story."

"Make sure you mention my role in it," Toby said. "And I suppose you'd better mention my brave assistants."

"Ye-es." Clarissa crooked an eyebrow as they turned into Mayflower Lane, then pulled up so they could pause and watch. The Magick Muffin was open for business and was doing a brisk trade. A few couples were sitting at tables on the pavement and there was a constant stream of people in and out of the door. Those who came out were, without exception, clutching paper carriers full of goodies.

Toby gazed up at Clarissa. "I'm famished."

She looked down at him. "Are you?" She knew exactly what was coming.

"Any chance of a sammich?"

"What flavour sammich would you like?"

Toby recalled the ham hock sammich that had never made it to his belly. He would have liked to try it, but the circumstances of its loss and the adventure afterwards had put him off. He needed something that made him feel warm inside. Nurtured. "Cheese."

"On its own?" Clarissa sounded surprised. "Is that your favourite?"

"It's my favourite favourite," he said.

COMING SOON

FANCY READING MORE OF TOBY'S ADVENTURES?

Grimly Fiendish: Spellbound Hound Magic and Mystery Book 9

Persecuting witches? Didn't that fall out of fashion in the seventeenth century?

Toby has always imagined so.

Why then is his great friend Mabel the hedge witch —a witch who actually lives in a hedge—coming in for so much strife from her local community?

That would be because a popular young man has been found dead and all the signs indicate a ritualistic murder.

When the police fail to identify a suspect, the locals need somewhere to pin the blame and therefore scapegoat poor Mabel. From the tone of the letters to the local newspaper, and the posts on Facebook, anyone would think Britain was returning to a time of burning and pillorying!

When Mabel's elderly cat Merrybutton reaches out in anguish, spellbound hound Toby can't refuse. There's something grimly fiendish at work here and Toby will need all of his cunning, wiles, magic and sass to get to the bottom of it and unearth the killer!

Available from April 2025

ALSO BY JEANNIE WYCHERLEY

Spellbound Hound

(*in reading order*)

Ain't Nothing but a Pound Dog: Spellbound Hound Magic and Mystery Book 1

A Curse, a Coven and a Canine: Spellbound Hound Magic and Mystery Book 2

Bark Side of the Moon: Spellbound Hound Magic and Mystery Book 3

Master of Puppies: Spellbound Hound Magic and Mystery Book 4

Dem Bones, Dem Bones: Spellbound Hound Magic and Mystery Book 5

Born to be Styled: Spellbound Hound Magic and Mystery Book 6

Up, Pup and Away: Spellbound Hound Magic and Mystery Book 7

Another One Bites the Crust: Spellbound Hound Magic and Mystery Book 8

Grimly Fiendish: Spellbound Hound Magic and Mystery Book 9 (Available April 29th 2025)

More than a Feline: Spellbound Hound Magic and Mystery Book 10 (Available Autumn 2025)

The Complete Wonky Inn Series

(*in chronological reading order*)

The Wonkiest Witch: Wonky Inn Book 1

The Ghosts of Wonky Inn: Wonky Inn Book 2

Weird Wedding at Wonky Inn: Wonky Inn Book 3

The Witch Who Killed Christmas: Wonky Inn Christmas Special

Fearful Fortunes and Terrible Tarot: Wonky Inn Book 4

The Mystery of the Marsh Malaise: Wonky Inn Book 5

The Mysterious Mr Wylie: Wonky Inn Book 6

The Great Witchy Cake Off: Wonky Inn Book 7

Vengeful Vampire at Wonky Inn: Wonky Inn Book 8

Witching in a Winter Wonkyland: A Wonky Inn Christmas Cozy Special

A Gaggle of Ghastly Grandmamas: Wonky Inn Book 9

Magic, Murder and a Movie Star: Wonky Inn Book 10

O' Witchy Town of Whittlecombe: A Wonky Inn Christmas Cozy Special

Judge, Jury and Jailhouse Rockcakes: Wonky Inn Book 11

A Midsummer Night's Wonky: Wonky Inn Book 12

Halloween Heebie-Geebies: Wonky Inn Book 13

Owl I want for Witchmas is Hoo: A Wonky Inn Christmas Cozy Mystery

Oh Mummy!: Wonky Inn Book 14

Pieces of Hate: Wonky Inn Book 15

The Faery of Witchmas Past: A Wonky Inn Christmas Cozy Special

Wonkytonk Witch: Wonky Inn Book 16

A Wonky Apprentice: Wonky Inn Book 17

A Barbarous Band of Blood Brothers: Wonky Inn Book 18

The Witchy Wood and the Weirdly Wyse: Wonky Inn Book 19 (November 29th 2024)

Wonderland Detective Agency

Dead as a Dodo: Wonderland Detective Agency Book 1

The Rabbit Hole Murders: Wonderland Detective Agency Book 2

Tweedledumb and Tweedledie: Wonderland Detective Agency Book 3

The Curious Incident at the Pig and Pepper: Wonderland Detective Agency Book 4

A Tragic Tea Party: Wonderland Detective Agency Book 5

The Pool of Tears: Wonderland Detective Agency Book 6

Into the Labyrinth: Wonderland Detective Agency Book 7 (Release TBC 2025)

The Municipality of Lost Souls

Midnight Garden: The Extra Ordinary World Novella Series Book 1

Beyond the Veil

Crone

A Concerto for the Dead and Dying

Deadly Encounters: A collection of short stories

Keepers of the Flame: A love story

With Peter Alderson Sharp

The Creature from the Grim Mire: A humorous Sci-fi, Time Travel and Alien Contact Mystery

Non-Fiction

Losing my best Friend: Thoughtful support for those affected by dog bereavement or pet loss

Follow Jeannie Wycherley

Buy me a coffee

Find out more at on the website

Or visit her on Facebook for her fiction

Follow Jeannie on Instagram (for bears and books)

See Jeannie on Tiktok @jeanniewycherley

Sign up for Jeannie's newsletter on her website